# The Gambler and the Law

Blamed for the murder of a prominent politician, gambler Dan Freemont is forced to flee Nebraska. Pursued by the real killer's henchmen he arrives at the small Wyoming town of Beecher Gulch where he hopes a planned rendezvous with a US Marshal will prove his innocence. But settlers are being attracted to the area and a conflict is developing between the newcomers and Carl Benton, the cattle king of the territory.

Mistaken for a town-taming lawman brought in to oppose the cattlemen, Dan is soon involved in the dispute and becomes a target for Benton's gunmen. As the fight builds to a climax, Dan's Nebraskan pursuers begin to close in on Beecher Gulch.

# The Gambler and the Law

Will DuRey

**A Black Horse Western**
ROBERT HALE

© Will DuRey 2016
First published in Great Britain 2016

ISBN 978-0-7198-1918-6

The Crowood Press
The Stable Block
Crowood Lane
Ramsbury
Marlborough
Wiltshire SN8 2HR

www.crowood.com

Robert Hale is an imprint
of The Crowood Press

Printed and bound in Great Britain by
CPI Antony Rowe, Chippenham and Eastbourne

# CHAPTER ONE

Dan Freemont left the room reflecting on the merits of a private poker party, especially when the other players were rich men for whom the get-together was mainly an opportunity to exchange business gossip and arrange deals that would make them richer. For Dan, gambling *was* business, and this night his business had boomed. Surreptitiously he pressed his right arm to his side, giving himself the satisfaction of feeling the thick wad of notes stored in an inner jacket pocket.

His inclusion in the game had been a matter of chance, the result of an encounter that afternoon with a man he'd met on a Mississippi river boat some years earlier. Robert Halliday was a magnate of industry, the owner of two mines and with stockholdings in the Union Pacific railway. In those days, when working the river boats, Dan had passed himself off as a land speculator, a common enough enterprise for a Northerner in the Southern states shortly after war, one for which regular attendance in the gambling salon was almost *de rigueur*. In keeping with that characterization he had told Robert Halliday that he was now seeking out suitable territory for a Chicago-based consortium intent on establishing a beef empire, either here in Nebraska or further west in Wyoming. The fact that his intended destination was even further north, Virginia City in Montana where gold was still being dug out of the ground, he kept to himself. It had never been his policy to leave a forwarding address because men who lost money at cards often wanted to get it back and weren't fussy how they got it.

Being a gambler, he'd learned, was all about bluff, being able to persuade people to believe what you wanted them to believe, and he was good at it. So, although he had no first-hand knowledge of the cattle business, he figured that he had learned enough while sitting around card tables with ranchers, cowboys and cattle buyers to be convincing on the subject, especially as none of the other three men who would be present had any direct connection with ranching. One of them, he was informed by Robert Halliday, would be the next governor of Nebraska.

Dan had seen banners and posters for both Republican and Democrat nominees ever since he'd arrived in Scottsbluff but, being a visitor, of course he wasn't eligible to vote, so he had taken little interest in the displays. He didn't know which candidate was favourite nor to which one Robert Halliday referred, but he was soon informed. A landslide victory was pre-dicted for the Republican candidate, Jason Whalley, and it was in his suite of rooms at the Minatare Hotel that they had gathered after dinner.

It had been a pleasant night, the game extending well beyond midnight with an abundance of brandy and cigars to accompany the cards and political conversation so that the hours swiftly passed. Dan had been introduced, welcomed and questioned about his affairs as a matter of course; politics apart on this occasion, business deals and money were the only eligible topics of conversation for such an assembly. With deft phrases that said neither too much nor too little, Dan was able to imply a degree of personal wealth and financial connection that satisfied their unsuspecting inquisitiveness. Although he presented a pleasant, carefree personality to those in the room, his attention never wandered from the cards. He was careful not to over-indulge in the available alcohol and smoked only his own slim coronas. His winning habit drew a comment or two but, for men who had drawn great wealth to themselves, their losses engendered no greater response than the raising of an eyebrow or the need to splash more brandy into their crystal goblet. Only Jason Whalley, Dan thought, had shown inquisitiveness at his good fortune. Twice, Dan had caught the would-be governor watching him, as though knowing he was not what he pretended to be.

The game ended suddenly. Gatt Hardin, Jason Whalley's aide, entered the room, drew his boss aside and, accompanied by some whispered comments, showed him a crumpled sheet of paper. On sight, they were unlikely colleagues; Whalley big-boned, handsome and groomed to the standard required of a prospective governor, listened to the urgent words of the other, a lanky, unfriendly man with a pock-marked face and dark, cold eyes that seemed incapable of showing humour. Dan had seen men like him before, usually employed as instruments of violence by pimps and waterside saloon-keepers.

'You must excuse me, gentlemen,' Whalley announced, 'a matter of business which I must conclude tonight. It has been a pleasure meeting you and I'm sure I can count on your support at next month's election.'

Hardin went into an adjoining room while Whalley, still clutching the paper he'd been given, hovered near the door, obviously anxious to join his colleague but maintaining his role as gracious host until all his guests had departed. A noise from the other room caught everyone's attention: a scuffle, a chair falling and a grunt or stifled complaint. Jason Whalley laughed it off, joking that Gatt Hardin must have had too much to drink..

Dan and Robert Halliday were the last to leave. As they stepped into the corridor they saw that two men were lounging against the wall outside the door to the adjoining room. One was young, some inches short of six feet tall but broad across the shoulders; he had fair hair but his most distinguishing feature was his top lip, which had an awkward twist, as though it had been torn and not healed properly, branding him with a permanent scowl.

The other man was older, with untidy hair and dark, heavy-lidded eyes. Neither man was dressed in a city manner; they looked rough but vigilant, carefully watching Dan and Robert as they took the stairs down to the lower floor.

It was then that Dan pressed his arm to his side, felt the comfort of the money but, in the same moment, realized that he had forgotten the pocket-box in which he kept his cigars. It was a favourite which, when hc'd produced it, had been admired by the other players. Franklin Peasgood, he recalled, a worthy of Scottsbluff whose good opinion Jason Whalley seemed eager to obtain, had taken one of the cigars, then put the case on the table beside his tumbler and chips. When the next hand had been dealt Dan's concentration had returned to the cards and the cigars had slipped from his mind. At the abrupt end to the game he had been concerned solely with cashing in his pile of chips for a bundle of banknotes. Reluctant to abandon the box that was something of a talisman for him, Dan stopped on the stairs and looked back to the balcony. The two men who had been lounging there were now going into the room adjoining the one in which the game had been played. The opportunity was there to collect his possession, so he said goodnight to Robert Halliday and while the other descended the stairs he stepped quickly back to the upper floor.

Quietly, he opened the door. A cautious peer inside told him that the room they'd been using was now unoccupied. However, the door to the adjoining room was ajar and voices from beyond it carried to him. Not hesitating, not wanting his return to be witnessed or misinterpreted as an act of spying on a prominent politician, he crossed to the table and collected the dark, ebony box he was seeking. He plucked it from the table, pushed it into the inner pocket alongside the bundle of money and was about to depart when something caught his eye. On the table, crumpled into an awkward ball, was the paper that Gatt Hardin had shown Jason Whalley.

By nature Dan Freemont was inquisitive, and a good gambler stored knowledge, for who knew when it would be useful and provide an advantage. Politics wasn't his forte but, despite the gracious manner in which he'd brought the evening to an end, it was clear that Jason Whalley had been discomfited by what he'd been shown. If it had a bearing on the upcoming election, then perhaps, for Dan, there was profit in it. Slowly, so as to minimize its rustle, he unravelled the paper. It was a Wanted poster, copies of which had been prominent across Kansas, Missouri and Arkansas in the early months after the end of the war. The face depicted was broad and from under a Confederate hat thick hair hung down to the man's shoulders. The lower part of his face was completely covered by an unkempt beard and moustache and his narrow eyes were topped by bushy brows. The printed name was Archie Baker, a renegade whose band had terrorized the mid-states fourteen years earlier, but along the bottom of the poster another name had been scribbled: This is Jason

Whalley.

For a moment, Dan stared at the picture. He knew it was a good likeness of the man whose acts of murder and robbery had made him one of the most feared gang leaders in the post-war years because one night they had been separated only by the width of a card table. It had happened in a Mexican town in 1867; Dan's wanderlust had, briefly, taken him across the Rio Grande and by chance found him in the town where Archie Baker had taken refuge from the American forces that had been closing in on him. Their paths had crossed for only the one night but Dan always remembered the air of menace that hung around the man. Every look, every movement was laden with suspicion and threat. Now, he wondered if the pink and pampered clean-shaven politician whose hospitality he'd enjoyed in this room earlier could be the same man.

Almost fourteen years had passed since that meeting and although the man he'd met this night matched him in height, the sparseness of flesh that characterized the hunted man was totally absent in the politician. It was clear that Jason Whalley had been living on the best of the land and the absence of facial hair and trimmed eyebrows showed a face that was fuller and a smile more friendly. Dan tried to imagine the younger face without a beard and at the same time was remembering the looks that Jason Whalley had thrown in his direction. Had he recognized Dan? It seemed unlikely, for their time together in Mexico had been brief and unexceptional other than that Dan had won big that night.

Then his musings were interrupted. While studying the poster he'd become aware that the conversation in the other room had taken on another tenor, it had become louder and the voices were heavy with anger and threat. He wasn't sure how many people were in the other room but just as he made the decision that it was time to leave the dull sound of a punch and an accompanying grunt reached him. The delivery of another punch was followed by the sound of a body crashing to the floor.

'Where did you get it?' someone asked, but there was no answer to the question.

Dan had no desire to become involved in the events that were unfolding in the other room; political machinations he would leave to others. He began to move towards the door that would take him back on to the balcony; he was halfway through the door when his departure was interrupted. The sound of a scuffle reached him and someone cursed; then suddenly the adjoining door, which had been ajar, was thrust open with such force that it crashed against the wall with a resounding crack. A man, not young, his thinning hair disturbed, blood seeping from his battered nose, dashed through. His eyes were bulging with fear and they fixed themselves on Dan Freemont. Dan could see a plea in his gaze and the necessary words beginning to form on his lips, but two gunshots sounded and the man jerked forward in his flight. Blood erupted from his chest as he was pitched on to the floor.

Framed in the doorway, smoking pistol in his

hand, Jason Whalley looked down on his victim. For a moment everything was still, then the politician raised his eyes and saw Dan Freemont with the Wanted poster in his hand. No words were exchanged but none were necessary for Whalley's intention to be understood. He began to raise the pistol again, Dan Freemont his new target.

Dan moved more quickly than he had ever done before, dashing into the corridor as a bullet gouged a lump of timber out of the doorway's stanchion. He could hear the commotion he'd left behind: curses and calls to get him, together with the stamp of running feet. Although the obvious route to escape the building was down the stairs to the foyer he knew that they were barred to him. The other door to the suite was at their head and he would be running into the arms of his pursuers. Instinctively, it seemed, he turned the other way, dashing along the corridor, not really sure that there was any sanctuary to be found.

Suddenly, on his right, a door opened. A man, in night-time attire, stepped into the corridor. Clearly, he had been disturbed by the gunshots and curiosity had brought him from his room to investigate. Two hands crashed into his chest and sent him sprawling, yelling in protest, along the corridor.

Dan Freemont darted into the bedroom and slammed the door behind him. A woman, clutching the bedclothes to her chest, shrieked but Dan ignored her. Swiftly he crossed to the window, opened it and looked out into the darkness. Indistinguishable though the extent of the drop was, he knew it to be substantial but he also knew that he had little choice but to commit himself to it. As he plunged down, he prayed that he would land without injury. He rolled as his feet hit the ground and in a moment he was up and running. From somewhere above a gun was fired; the bullet passed him in the darkness of the alley.

Under his left arm Dan carried a gun, but he had never considered himself a gunfighter. There had been times when he'd drawn it, even used it on a couple of occasions, and he was as accurate as any man when separated from his target by the width of a card table. At that moment, however, his only thought was to put as great a distance as possible between himself and Jason Whalley's people. The lack of light in the alley was a benefit to Dan. Another couple of shots were fired in his direction but the bullets were wide and high of their target, making it clear that the shooters had fired in hope rather than with a clear view of their target.

Stooping as he ran, Dan reached the end of the block and turned into another narrow alley between buildings, which led him away from the hotel. Momentarily, he experienced a sense of safety; he doubted if any of those who had fired at him from the windows of the upper rooms would risk the drop that he'd undertaken; he had done it only to preserve his life. Behind him he could still hear voices and he guessed that a hunt would soon be organized. At that moment he had only a vague idea where his current route would lead him and, more troubling, even less idea of what to do to ensure his safety. Ahead of him he could see the line of grey light that heralded an opening on to a major thoroughfare. Reducing his pace to a brisk walk he hurried towards it.

Suddenly, behind him, he heard a sound. Someone was running. Pressing himself against the building to his right he peered back into the blackness. By then his pursuer, too, had stopped. Dan waited. The distant voices of those who had fired at him from the hotel reached him; their words were indistinct but Dan guessed that whoever was on the ground was receiving instructions to continue the chase. After a moment a distant movement caught his attention and with careful concentration he discerned two figures. Judging them to be about fifty yards away he knew that he couldn't afford to delay any longer. At that distance it was unlikely that they would hit him with a pistol shot, but if he tarried they would soon be within range.

Breaking cover, stooping as he had done previously, Dan made a dash for the main thoroughfare. A loud report echoed down the alley as a whistling bullet passed inches over his head. To his alarm, at least one of his pursuers was armed with a rifle, which put him in greater danger. Another bullet, closer to him than the first, caused him to stumble as he emerged into the more open main street. He went down but had the sense to roll away to his left so that he was out of the direct line of shots from the men in the alley.

The street was empty of people although the faint sound of music reached him from an establishment visible off to his right where light shone from its windows. Dan estimated that the saloon was almost 200 yards away and knew that he had no hope of reaching it before his hunters emerged from the alley. In the moonlight they wouldn't fail to kill him.

With long strides he ran, heading for an offset, opposite alley which he hoped would lead to a warren of passageways in which he could evade those behind. Halfway across the street, however, he had a change of heart. As the footfalls of his hunters reached his ears more loudly, indicating that they were closer than he'd hoped, a hiding-place presented itself. What he did was risky but so was running in the dark without any idea of where he was going. He turned around, dropped to the ground and rolled. A water trough beside a hitching rail had been raised above the ground by means of wooden blocks at either end. There was room enough for Dan to roll underneath, where he hoped that in the darkness his black hat and coat would aid his invisibility and his pursuers would pass him by.

Dan was breathing hard as he scrambled beneath the wooden trough; if they found him he knew that they would kill him. With that thought in mind he reached for the pistol in his shoulder holster and it was at that moment that he realized that he still clutched the Wanted poster he'd picked up in Jason Whalley's room. With the minimum of movement he pushed it up the sleeve of his jacket, then lay still with his pistol cocked in readiness.

'Where is he?' The question was asked in a low,

urgent voice. The men had stopped running as soon as they'd emerged on to the moonlit street.

'Probably over there, somewhere. Those alleyways lead to the courthouse and sheriff's office on Montrose Street.'

'Do we go after him?'

'I guess so. I'll follow him through the alleys while you go around. We've got him trapped.'

'We don't know who he is or what he looks like.' There was a hint of uncertainty in the first man's voice. 'We don't even know what he's done. We can't just kill any man who's on the street.'

'Who's going to be on the street at this hour?'

'The Irishman's bar is still open down the street. Do you think he headed for that?'

'He went off to his left when he left the alley. He's over there somewhere. Somewhere between here and Montrose Street. Let's go.'

Dan Freemont had listened to the conversation with mixed feelings. He was pleased that they intended to continue the search among the alleyways across the street, but it troubled him to learn that if he tried to report what he knew to the sheriff he ran the risk of running into Whalley's men. He watched their feet, waiting for them to go their separate ways, which would give him the opportunity to find a more secure hiding-place.

'Hey!' The call was made by a third voice. 'Where is he?'

'Somewhere over there. What has he done?'

'Killed Henry Garland.'

'We planned to flush him out on to Montrose Street.'

The newcomer snorted with amusement. 'That would be convenient,' he said. 'Gatt's on his way to the sheriff's office to get the law's help.'

'I reckon Mr Whalley can count on that. The law has certainly made the most of Mr Whalley's hospitality while he's been in Scottsbluff.'

'Somebody will have to sober up Sheriff Blain. Last time I saw him he wasn't able to help anyone, including himself.'

Those words produced a snigger of laughter but the newcomer put a stop to it.

'Sheriff Blain will do exactly as he's told. Mr Whalley will see to that.'

Dan Freemont remained under the trough for several minutes after the trio had departed. He reholstered his pistol, brushed down his clothes, then proceeded along the street towards the town limits with a troubled mind. Jason Whalley, it appeared, was accusing him of the hotel killing and the sheriff was in Whalley's pocket. If they got him into a jail cell it was unlikely that he would get out alive. For now, his only chance of survival was to get out of town.

# CHAPTER TWO

Although he'd arrived in Scottsbluff by train, Dan Freemont ruled that out as a means of escape. The platform was probably under observation by Whalley's men. His departure was now a matter of urgency and secrecy and a horse was his immediate need. So, using every bit of cover available to him, he made his way to the town's southern limit. Although his general familiarity with Scottsbluff's layout was slight, he did know the location of a livery stable. He had hired a buggy and team there one day when the girl in the restaurant he frequented accepted his invitation to a picnic along the river. He'd been given a pretty, prancing pair of animals that befitted the occasion, but now his need was for a sturdy and speedy beast that would carry him far away to safety.

While he made his way towards the stable he considered his next move. By quitting Scottsbluff he knew that he was adding credence to Jason Whalley's charge that he had killed the man in the hotel, but if he stayed he knew that his counter-claim would be disbelieved and he would be convicted of murder. There was nothing to be gained by staying; he had to tell his story in another town and trust that the truth would clear him of being a cold-blooded killer.

The problem, of course, when he reached another town was whom to tell. There weren't many law officers of his acquaintance who would believe the story of a gambler against that of a politician. He hadn't been forced to leave any town and some town marshals and sheriffs had been as friendly with him as they were with any other stranger, but it didn't mean they held him in the kind of esteem that would be bestowed on a pillar of society like a visiting governor-elect.

In the end he decided that Mark Clement was the best person to whom he should disclose his story. They weren't friends, exactly, but they had shared meals, downed drinks and exchanged stories in as sociable a manner as Dan had known with any man. Mark Clement was a newspaper man: reporter, editor, publisher and printer of the *Bugle* in Ogallala. He, Dan figured, would listen to his story and offer unbiased advice. Moreover, Ogallala was not too distant. With a good horse under him he could be there within two days.

By the time Dan reached his destination  its large doors, as he'd excpected, were closed but he wasn't unduly dismayed. In large towns stables, like hotels, often had night staff on site. He knocked at the wicket door and waited. After a few moments he was rewarded by a glow of light reaching out from under the big doors, followed by the rattle of the latch as the smaller door was opened. The man inside had the appearance of one about to fall asleep or who had just been awakened. He was hatless, wore cross-belted jeans over a red-chequered shirt and carried a lantern, which he held high so that its light illuminated Dan's face.

'I need a horse,' announced Dan, as he stepped into the huge barnlike structure where most of the two dozen stalls were occupied.

'Is one of these yours?' asked the stableman, looking along the double row of horses.

'No. I need one of yours. And a saddle.'

'You buying it?'

Dan pressed his arm against his side, gratified that he'd won a pocketful of money because he couldn't go back to his room for the few possessions he'd brought with him to Scottsbluff.

'Yes,' he said, wanting to hurry the business along so that he could be quickly on the road to Ogallala.

'I'm not sure which ones I'm allowed to sell,' muttered the man as he walked deeper into the stable. 'Can't it wait until the morning?'

'No.' Dan followed, casting an eye over the animals they passed.

'Those horses are just stabled here,' the man told him. 'Ours are at the end of the row.'

Near the rear doors, at right angles to those they'd walked past, were half a dozen stalls in which curious animals turned their heads to study those responsible for disturbing their rest. While the stableman lit a couple of lanterns, Dan stepped closer to the horses.

A big red animal caught his eye immediately and he asked the price.

'Good horse,' said the stableman. 'I'm not sure the owner wants to sell him. It's his favourite.'

Dan didn't want to waste time haggling. 'Two hundred,' he said, withdrawing the bundle of money as he spoke. 'Horse and saddle.'

It was a fair price, both buyer and stableman knew it, but the latter muttered again that he wasn't sure if the animal was for sale. To persuade him, Dan produced another fifty-dollar bill and pushed all the money into the man's hand. Then, after selecting a rig from a rack of equipment, he saddled up and was ready to leave.

'I'll open a door for you,' the stableman said, and hurried ahead.

As Dan reached the opened door he heard voices: the man was in conversation with someone outside the stable.

'Comings and goings at all hours,' he was saying and Dan was instantly alert. He knew it could be an innocent cowboy seeking his horse for the journey home, but equally it could be one of Jason Whalley's men searching for him. He would have withdrawn, gone back into the deeper reaches of the stable until he'd satisfied himself of the newcomer's intentions, but he wasn't given that opportunity. The man was already stepping past the stableman and peering along the aisle between the stalls.

For a moment, both men remained motionless as they observed each other. Then, with barely the passage of a split second, both reacted. The young man with the contorted lip dropped his right hand to his hip, his fingers tightened around the butt of his pistol and his thumb pressed back its hammer. Fortunately Dan had been the first to move and had hurled himself forward to attack his enemy. Before the other could draw and fire his weapon, Dan's fist hit him full in the face, causing him to fall stretched full length on the floor.

Diving forward, Dan landed on his opponent's chest. His left arm reached down to prevent the other man drawing his pistol from its holster. With his right fist he tried to land another blow on his opponent's jaw but his effort was resisted. Although knocked off his feet, the younger man had been less affected by Dan's punch than was to be expected and he began twisting violently, using his knee in an effort to wind his assailant.

For a few seconds they rolled on the floor, the young man desperately struggling to draw his gun and Dan attempting to gain some sort of advantage by which he could disarm his opponent. Punches were exchanged but with most of the efforts of both men focused on the tussle for the gun, they had little effect.

Finding a surprising surge of strength, the young man with the twisted lip rolled over, causing Dan to crash against the stout wooden prop of the nearest stall. The impact momentarily stunned him, allowing the young man to wrest his right hand free so that he was able to pull out the pistol. Instantly Dan recovered. His left hand clutched for the other's gun hand and twisted it so that the bullet, when it was fired, flew through the open doorway into the darkness of the night. The nearest horse, already startled by the atmosphere of violence, shied, neighed and kicked against the timbers of its stall.

Having regained his grip on the young man's right wrist and in an effort to force him to drop his weapon, Dan dashed the gun hand against the ground. When that failed, amid grunts and swapped blows and with a determination to keep the barrel of the pistol pointed away from himself, he struggled to his knees, then to his feet, pulling the other up after him. The young man failed in an attempt to knee Dan in the groin and that proved to be his final thrust in the skirmish. Realizing that they were too close for the punches he was throwing with his right hand to have any serious effect, Dan changed tactics. He grabbed the young man's chin and swung him so that his head collided with one of the stall posts. The effect on his opponent was more one of surprise than pain but it gave Dan the opportunity to gain a better hold. When he rammed his opponent's head against the post a second time it stunned him. Dan could feel the other man sag and knew that one more blow would put an end to the fight. He was right. The young man's eyes widened, then glazed over as his knees buckled and the gun fell from his hands.

Dan kicked the weapon deep into the stable as he let his opponent fall to the ground. He gathered the reins of the big red he'd recently bought, led it outside and put a foot in the stirrup. The sound of running and shouting reached his ears. He looked down the street and saw three men approaching hastily, calling for him to stop. Dan swung into the saddle and turned the horse on to the road south. Behind him the shouting continued, then shots were fired, but the horse was running now and the road ahead was free.

Jason Whalley received the news of Dan Freemont's escape with cold fury.

'Why are you here?' he demanded to know of Gatt Hardin. 'Why aren't you giving chase. I want that gambler caught.' He cast a look at Sheriff Blain, who had returned to the hotel with Hardin and added, 'Caught and punished by the law. Henry Garland was not only a dear friend but also a pillar of the state of Nebraska.'

'The men returned to collect their horses and to find out if you had any special instructions.'

'Find him,' insisted Whalley. Then, as the first fluster of the setback dwindled and the realization that a strategy for the capture of Dan Freemont was required, he spoke again. His voice was lower and calmer, the tone authoritative, befitting a man who would make momentous decisions if he became governor.

'He went south, you say?'

'That's right,' Gatt Hardin told him. 'He'll have an hour's start on us by the time everyone is saddled up.'

'Where will that take him?' Whalley's question was directed at Sheriff Blain.

'Kimball, Pine Bluffs, then across the state border

into Colorado. If he turns east the nearest towns are Ogallala and Julesburg. Going west would take him into Wyoming territory.'

Whalley knew that Dan Freemont's plan would be to spill his story to the law, but he wouldn't want to tell it to some hick-town constable, so that ruled out Kimball and Pine Bluffs. If he had any sense, mused Whalley, he'd quit Nebraska but to reach Greeley or Denver in Colorado or even Cheyenne in Wyoming would involve rough riding through rocky hills. It would take several days to reach those towns and, he guessed, Freemont would want to tell his story and declare his innocence as soon as possible.

'I reckon he'll head for Julesburg,' he announced, 'or Ogallala. How long will it take him to reach either of those places?'

'Best part of two days,' replied Sheriff Blain, 'but I can send telegraph messages to all the law offices around the state. With everyone on the lookout he'll soon be caught and he can be brought back here for trial.'

'Good,' said Whalley. 'Wake up the telegraph operator and get those messages sent now. Let us make sure we close every avenue of escape for him.'

As Sheriff Blain left to do Whalley's bidding the politician spoke to Gatt Harding.

'Freemont must be caught and preferably before he reaches another town,' he said, 'but make sure that he doesn't survive to stand trial. Don't come back here until he's dead.'

*

Dark clouds were threatening a summer downpour when Dan Freemont cantered into Ogallala. Consequently few people were abroad that afternoon and those who were showed no interest in the stranger on the big red horse. Like all men who travelled, it was Dan's usual practice to tend to the needs of his horse first when arriving at journey's end, but on this occasion he broke that habit. The horse had served him well and after the initial flight which had left Scottsbluff twenty miles in his wake he had settled into a pattern of running and walking. This had conserved the animal's stamina and had also ensured that the gap was maintained between himself and any pursuers. He had had no food since quitting Scottsbluff and the horse had had to be content with grass, but neither of them was the worse for that. Now, though, they were both tired and Dan knew that he would require a fresh horse if, after talking with Mark Clement, he had to continue riding.

Mark Clement was alone when Dan walked into his office. When he recognized his visitor he dropped his pencil, jumped to his feet and hurried to lock the door and pull down the blind.

'What are you doing here? Has anyone seen you?'

Surprised by the newspaperman's behaviour, the gambler shook his head.

'I came straight here. I didn't even stable my horse.'

'A good thing too. Harvey at the stable would have reported your arrival to the sheriff if he'd seen you.'

'Why would he do that?'

Mark Clement grabbed a newssheet from a nearby table and handed it to Dan. The headline announced the murder of Henry Garland. Dan didn't have to read far into the story to find his name and his denunciation as a cold-blooded killer.

'I didn't do this,' he told Mark Clement. 'I was there but I didn't kill anyone. How did you get this story so quickly?'

'The sheriff received a telegraph message from his counterpart in Scottsbluff. Apparently every law office in the state has received one.'

'Then I'm in more trouble than I knew. I need your help.' When the newspaperman remained silent Dan stressed his innocence. 'I promise you, I didn't kill that man. I don't even know who he is.'

'Henry Garland was a prominent Republican. He was acting as political agent for Jason Whalley's push to be governor of the state. I knew him. He was a good man.'

'Mark, I didn't kill that man. I witnessed his murder and the man who killed him was Jason Whalley.'

Disbelief was the first reaction that passed across the newspaperman's features, but when he examined Dan's face he could detect no hint of deception. Dan Freemont's reputation was that of a self-interested man but there had never been any suggestion that he would murder in cold blood.

'Can you prove that? Were there any other witnesses?'

'Yes, there were other witnesses but all of them are Whalley's men. They'll swear that I killed him. They tried to kill me in Scottsbluff and it's possible that they are on my trail.'

'Tell me everything,' said Mark Clement. So Dan told him about the poker night, its abrupt end and his return to the room to gather up his cigar case. Producing the Wanted poster he assured Mark that that was the reason for Henry Garland's death.

Mark Clement pursed his lips when he opened the Wanted poster and revealed the face of Archie Baker.

'Haven't heard of him for years. Thought he'd gone to South America or Australia. Could it be the same man?'

The question had been nothing more than a thought spoken aloud but Dan picked up on it and confirmed that in his opinion it could be true and, as evidence, recounted his meeting with Archie Baker in Mexico some years ago.

'My advice,' Mark said, 'is to get out of Nebraska as quickly as possible. You need to tell your story to an independent party, someone who will investigate it while you remain somewhere safe.'

'Can you suggest anyone?'

'I can get word to the federal marshal's office in St Louis and arrange a meeting on neutral territory. My suggestion would be Wyoming. It's not yet in the Union so they can't arrest you for a crime in Nebraska.'

He walked across to a map on the wall and traced a line that was a representation of the Union Pacific

Railroad. After a moment he stabbed his finger at a certain spot.

'There,' he said, 'Beecher Gulch, a one-street town west of Cheyenne. No one will look for you there. When requested, trains stop there. Apart from that I don't suppose anything ever happens. Wait there, Dan, until you're contacted by a US marshal.'

The newspaperman offered the gambler a room for the night but Dan refused. Mark's own freedom would have been threatened if he were caught harbouring a wanted criminal, but he did take advantage of a change of clothes, which Mark considered necessary. The full coat and frilled evening shirt he was wearing marked Dan for attention. The new wardrobe consisted of a heavy blue shirt, denim trousers and a short jacket. There was also a gunbelt into which Dan slid the Colt that had been housed in his shoulder holster.

While Dan changed into his new duds his host prepared a meal of ham and eggs, which were gratefully devoured. They exchanged horses and although the big red was the better of the two the benefit to Dan was that Mark's was in a stable behind the newspaper office, thus he was able to get astride and away without coming under the observation of any other citizen.

Dan left the alley that led from Mark Clement's stable on to Ogallala's main thoroughfare with a sense of confidence. In Wyoming he would be safe from prosecution by the law and he was sure that an independent investigation into the killing of Henry

Garland would clear his name.

He looked up at the sky and wondered how far he would get before the rain came. Urging the horse to a canter he headed south. It was only as he was passing the Red Garter saloon, where he'd spent many hours, that he realized he was heading in the direction of the sheriff's office. It was too late to turn back, such a manoeuvre would only draw attention to himself; all he could do was ride on and hope that the sheriff was indoors to avoid the coming rain. In fact, as he drew close, it appeared that the sheriff was engaged, because there was a cluster of mounts tied to the rail outside his office. Dan tugged down the brim of his black hat as he approached the building and turned in the saddle to present his back to anyone watching from the window.

He was directly opposite the door to the sheriff's office when it opened. Unable to resist a look in its direction, Dan was startled to see Gatt Hardin emerge. Hardin didn't see Dan, he was busy talking, casting words backwards to those that were behind. The second man was the young man with the twisted lip, the one with whom Dan had fought in the Scottsbluff stable. Their eyes met and for both recognition was immediate. With a yell the young man drew his gun and fired a shot in Dan's direction.

Instantly Dan thrust himself forward so that he was lying low along the horse's neck. Using voice, hands and spurs he put the beast under him to a gallop. Behind him, the reports from pistols cracked in the air but no bullets came close. He turned to look back along the street and saw the men climbing on to their mounts to give chase. There were five of them and they were yelling and spurring their horses in pursuit. Dan suspected that the men had ridden those horses all the way from Scottsbluff, which meant that they weren't likely to catch him on his fresh animal.

Once clear of the town limits he turned east and gave the horse its head. A gap was soon established. He rode east for several miles until he entered a densely wooded area. where he stopped, dismounted and concealed himself until his pursuers rode by. He remounted and rode back the way he had come, swung south to bypass Ogallala, then continued west towards Wyoming.

# CHAPTER THREE

From the bluff Dan Freemont surveyed the land he'd
left behind, the endless, treeless tract of green prairie
which was decorated with daubs of yellow, blue and
purple by the flowering Indian paintbrushes, western
columbine and fringed gentian. Under the cloudless
blue sky, the view was redolent of some Currier & Ives
prints he'd seen on his last visit to Pittsburgh, pictures
of a paradise designed to lure families to the unsettled
West. Stretching to a distant horizon, the terrain
looked flat and cultured, like the lawns surrounding
the Washington homes of prominent senators, but
it was an illusion, the eye tricked by the angle of view
and the magnitude of the vista. The ground he had
covered was uneven, its troughs and rises apparent now
only as irregular patches of dark and light. In places
the grass was as high as his horse's breast; if the breeze
had been strong enough it would have been rippling
like an ocean wave.

However, Dan hadn't paused at this point to admire
the scenery; his watchfulness had the same purpose

that every other look over his shoulder had had for the last seven days: to reassure himself that Jason Whalley's men weren't hot on his heels. Indeed, since eluding them outside Ogallala there had been no sign of pursuit. With each passing day he had become more certain that his hunters were searching for him in the wrong part of the country. Now that he was deep in Wyoming territory with the empty prairie behind him he was confident that he would not be discovered.

For now, his only concern was that the law authorities would not act on Mark Clement's information. It was, he had to admit, an unlikely tale, a wanted renegade using an alias to seek high public office, but Archie Baker had considered himself a general during the violence of that post-war era, so delusions about his status and abilities were not new. But would the marshal's office send someone to Beecher Gulch to negotiate, or would they want Dan to surrender himself to a trial in Scottsbluff? Apart from the old Wanted poster he had nothing to back up his story, and even that was scarcely evidence of his innocence or Whalley's guilt.

He took a drink of water from his canteen, then headed north at an easy pace. After the first day, when his plan had been to put as much distance as possible between himself and any pursuers, his progress had not been over-demanding on his horse. An injury to it might leave him afoot and alone in that isolated, unknown territory. Also, because he was not following an established trail, he'd had to establish his bearings by means of the small compass he carried. He'd quit

Ogallala with little more than a general idea of the route he needed to follow to reach Beecher Gulch. The previous day he'd run into a small cavalry patrol whose officer had directed him towards Cheyenne. That was a town that Dan intended to avoid, but its location provided markers that would guide him to Beecher Gulch. Now, if his calculations were correct, the North Platte on whose banks that town was sited, was not far ahead.

He had been riding west, parallel with the river, for almost an hour when he reined to a sudden halt. Unexpectedly, off to his left, a line of posts stretched away into the distance. A horse, harnessed between the shafts of a flat wagon, was grazing nearby. Catching the scent of Dan's mount it raised its head and snickered a welcome. Dan remained motionless, studying the area but neither sight nor sound reached him to betray the whereabouts of the owner of the rig. A silent minute passed; then, at a walk, Dan moved closer.

His first impression had been that the planted poles were awaiting the attachment of cross-planks to complete a fence, but as he approached he recognized his mistake. Between each post he discerned three silver strands of wire but it wasn't like any wire he'd seen before. Closer inspection revealed a regular pattern of sharp-pointed twists. This, Dan realized, was the barbed wire he'd read about. A fence strung with it was cheaper and quicker to erect than an all timber fence. It was proving popular with many land-owners too, but Dan figured that a man would have to be careful when working with it.

Now that he'd moved around the wagon he could see that a bundle of material had been tied with some of the wire and draped over the nearest completed section. Suddenly he realized that the bundle didn't consist solely of material. He jumped down and dashed to the assistance of the stricken man, but his haste was unnecessary. Apart from being bound with barbed wire, the man had been shot several times. There were bullet holes in his back and his shirt was soaked in his blood. Head shots had almost destroyed his face and his fair hair was matted with blood.

It took fifteen minutes to get the body on to the flatbed of the wagon, a difficult operation due in part to the weight of the victim but mainly because of the liberal use that had been made of the binding barbed wire. Dan's reward was a series of rips to his hands, arms and chest. He lashed his saddle horse to the wagon's tailboard and continued westwards, aware that this example of barbaric violence was a sure sign that civilization was close at hand.

Having travelled through Texas and beyond en route to Mexico, frontier towns were not unknown to Dan Freemont and his anticipation of Beecher Gulch was of a small community of simple buildings and limited resources. In fact, it was larger than he'd expected, boasting, in addition to an emporium which advertised hardware, provisions, grain and clothing on its exterior sign, a series of specialist shops such as a milliner, a gunsmith, a boot-maker and a barber.

There was a bank and a doctor, plus three saloons, two of which took paying guests. A blacksmith's forge and livery stable marked its southern limit, while the railroad passed to the north, where a small trackside building served as ticket and telegraph office. The jumble of buildings to left and right behind the main street were the homes of the residents which spread down to the river on one side and up a slope on the other. Each one was different, the site and size chosen at the whim of the owner. All were timber built, several being stout and permanent in appearance, while others were flimsy and seemed likely to be scattered far and wide with the arrival of the next strong wind.

But it had been several years since Dan had strayed from the growing circuit of cities and large towns where he plied his trade. In that time he had become accustomed to the sight of planned townscapes, street lighting and buildings with solid foundations, some of which were three and four storeys high. Simplicity he had expected but he was surprised by the grubbiness of the buildings and the dry-baked, dusty street which was barely two wagons wide and rutted. An air of impermanence hung about the town and was added to by the camp he passed before reaching the blacksmith's forge. Around twenty tarpaulin tents had been erected on the meadow where men, women and children lingered with no apparent purpose.

At first Dan's arrival in town didn't draw anything more than the usual questioning glance. The blacksmith watched from the open doors of his forge until the trundling wagon halted outside the sheriff's office in the centre of the street. By then Theo Dawlish, who owned the emporium and was busily brushing dust from the walkway outside his establishment, had taken note of the newcomer's arrival, and a couple of fellows who were gossiping outside a building that had no other legend than SALOON painted over its batwing doors stopped jawing. It was clear that those men had recognized the wagon and were curious about the driver. When Dan stepped down from the board and went into the sheriff's office they crossed the street to conduct their own investigation.

When Dan returned to the street he had the sheriff in tow. Fred Onslow was a couple of inches short of Dan's six feet and he walked unhurriedly. He looked up and down the street before walking around to the end of the wagon to examine its contents.

'It's Ben,' said one of the two men who had checked the body while Dan had been inside the sheriff's office. 'Ben Riddle. Look what they've done to him, Sheriff.'

The man who had spoken turned an accusing gaze on Dan Freemont. He was about thirty with a gaunt expression. His hands were large and grimed with his labour, his face was long, his nose wide and his eyes blue. Like his hands, his clothes were marked with signs of field work, his dark cord breeches were soiled at the knees and mud-marks showed on his faded blue shirt where he'd rubbed dirty hands.

'What are you going to do, Sheriff?'

Sheriff Onslow made no reply, instead he climbed

on to the wagon, knelt beside the corpse and touched the body in a manner that implied he was counting the bullets that had been fired into it. He grunted slightly as he tested the binding wire, the sound provoked by the barbarity of the deed.

'He's been murdered,' said the talkative bystander.

'You may not think much of me as a sheriff, Tom Keogh,' replied the sheriff as he climbed down, 'but even I didn't think he'd shot himself then wrapped himself up with wire.'

Tom Keogh wasn't abashed by Sheriff Onslow's sarcasm. 'What are you going to do about it?'

By this time Theo Dawlish had reached the wagon and the group was soon joined by Zach Hartnell, the blacksmith. Other people on the street, aware that something was amiss, were beginning to congregate.

'Let's get this body off the street,' said Sheriff Onslow. 'Tom, drive the wagon down to the undertaker's shop. Tell Sepp Lucas to do the best he can. Can't let Ben Riddle's wife see him like that.'

'Then what? What are you going to do about catching his murderer?' Tom Keogh's suspicious look at Dan Freemont wasn't lost on any among the gathering. A sigh escaped the sheriff's mouth.

'Did you kill that man?'' he asked Dan.

'No.'

'Didn't think you did.' He turned to Tom Keogh. 'Satisfied?' He carried on speaking before the other could reply. 'Don't suppose you are.' He held out his hand to Dan Freemont. 'Better let me see your gun.'

A quick examination revealed that one chamber was empty.

'The one under the hammer,' Dan explained. 'I've been travelling, didn't want to put a hole in my foot or my horse's belly.'

'Good figuring,' conceded the genial sheriff, sniffing the barrel of the weapon. He offered it to Tom Keogh. 'Hasn't been fired since Abe Lincoln was a lad,' he announced. 'Now, you and Luke do my bidding. Take the body down to Sepp Lucas and leave the matter to me.'

Tom Keogh looked ready to prolong the discussion but his friend was already up on the wagon's board. Without support for his agitation Keogh was forced to concede and with a last surly glare for Dan he followed the wagon down the street.

'This is a bad business, Fred.' The words were uttered by Theo Dawlish. 'What are you going to do?'

'Inform his wife.'

'I mean about his killing.'

'I know what you mean.'

'Is this the start? Will there be more killing?'

'It started when the first settler got off the train. Perhaps it started when the railway laid its line past our town. As for more killing, then your guess is as good as mine.'

Zach Hartnell, the blacksmith, indicated Dan.

'Who is this?' he asked.

'What did you say your name was?' enquired the sheriff.

'I didn't. It's Dan Bayles.' The lie had come readily to his lips. If the accusation attached to Dan Freemont had spread to Wyoming then his innocence of this killing would also be in doubt.

'Where did you find the body?'

'About five miles out of town. He was draped over a fence he'd been building.'

'A wire fence?'

'Sure.'

Theo Dawlish cursed. 'I knew it was a mistake to bring in that wire. Carl Benton made it clear he wouldn't let anybody fence the range.'

'Perhaps you'd ride with me,' the sheriff said to Dan, 'show me where you found him.'

Dan wasn't eager. 'I've been travelling for some time,' he said. 'I could do with filling my stomach.'

'I appreciate your need,' Sheriff Onslow told him, 'but there's a woman back there who doesn't know she's a widow. It would benefit me if I could break the news to her and see the spot where her husband died in one trip. If you could see your way clear to accompany me I'd willingly buy that meal you crave when we get back.'

Sheriff Onslow's whimsical manner amused Dan and he acceded to his request. However he wasn't duped by the easy-going lawman and harboured no illusion that he was anything other than an intelligent and resourceful peace-keeper. Within five minutes they were cantering back past the tents on the meadow towards the spot where Dan had found Ben Riddle's body. As they rode they exchanged information.

Since the defeat of Custer, four years earlier, the aftermath of which had virtually ended the Indian wars, the Northern territories had become ripe for settlement. Urged by government incentives, people were heading west to claim the free sections on which to farm and raise stock. Some still travelled overland in wagons but many more were taking advantage of the railroad and, with the trains passing the end of the town, Beecher Gulch had become one of the many dropping points along the Union Pacific's line. A handful of families now occupied strips of land around the town, had built their homes and planted their crops and the occupants of the tents on the meadow were the latest influx who would move out to their allotted strips when their equipment and provisions were delivered.

Of course, they faced opposition. Established cattle ranchers across the great grasslands opposed the loss of land that had been freely grazed by their beasts over the years, With the coming of the settlers and the planting of crops, fences were going up and, in some instances, access to water was being withheld. Carl Benton, whose Flying B was the predominant brand in the area around Beecher Gulch, had vowed that he would not lose an inch of land to the newcomers and that fences would be trampled down. Sheriff Onslow and the councilmen of Beecher Gulch, acting as a buffer between the two sides, were barely able to maintain peace.

'I need a deputy,' the lawman said, using his most disarming tone, as though hoping that Dan would apply for the position. 'Will you be staying long in Beecher Gulch?'

'I can't say for sure, but probably not. I hope to meet someone here, then I'll probably head for Viginia City.'

'You don't look like a prospector.'

'That's true,' conceded Dan but he was relieved of the need for more discussion because ahead of them was the low building constructed of timber and prairie sods that was the Riddle home.

Mrs Riddle watched the approaching horsemen with a mixture of pleasure and apprehension. The prospect of company, if only for a few minutes, excited her because she hadn't seen anyone apart from her husband for more than three weeks, but he wasn't here to receive them. He had been away all day and suddenly she was overcome by the sensation of being defenceless.

She wore a long, grey dress and a wide-brimmed hat which was tied to her head with a scarf fastened under her chin. She was tall and slim and although her hands were rough from incessant labour she had not yet suffered the heat of a full summer, which would crack her skin and age her twenty years before she'd lived another five. She stood erect, refraining from raising her hand to shade her eyes because there was no one she would recognize. These men were strangers and she hoped their intentions were good.

'Mrs Riddle,' one of them called, 'I'm Sheriff Onslow from Beecher Gulch and this is my associate, Dan Blayne. Is it all right if we step down a moment?'

Sarah Riddle smiled. Here was company she could

trust because she remembered seeing the sheriff on her last visit to the town.

She bore the news stoically until they departed, then she was alone with a hole in her soul. In the morning people from the town would arrive; women to comfort her, men to help her pack her belongings, but for now she was forlorn, an emptiness inside her as vast as that of the surrounding land.

They had followed the fence for more than a mile in the direction of the river until they reached the point where Dan had discovered the body. Sheriff Onslow dismounted and scanned the area. The ground was scuffed by hoof- and boot-marks and areas of flattened grass indicated that a scuffle had taken place. There was an abundance of drying splatters of blood, all of which, the lawman suspected, had been spilled from the dead man.

'We've got company,' Dan told him and gestured with his head to the other side of the river, where four horsemen had them under observation.

'Carl Benton's men,' the sheriff announced. He climbed back into the saddle. 'The one with the moustache is his foreman, Rod Westerway. To his right on the grey is Chas Tulley. A young hothead. I've had his company on several nights with only a few iron bars between us. Always looking for a fight. Thinks he's fast with a gun and he might be, so don't let him provoke you.'

'I don't intend to.'

'The other two are Patch Reid and Sim Taylor.'

The two parties watched each other for a few minutes, then the cowboys urged their ponies into the river and rode across.

'Rare to see you out of town, Sheriff,' said Rod Westerway. 'Must be something important to bring you so far.'

Before answering, the sheriff pushed his horse closer to the foreman. To give him room Dan turned sideways, thereby presenting a left profile to the new arrivals.

'A man was killed here today. A decent man, working for the betterment of himself and his family.'

Chas Tulley pushed his horse forward. 'You can't call anyone who fixes up a wire fence a decent man.'

'Shut up, Chas,' said Rod Westerway. Fred Onslow fixed his gaze on Chas Tulley.

'Who said he was stringing up wire?'

'Seems like the sort of a thing a man who got himself killed would be doing.' Tulley laughed, looking around at the other two riders as if expecting to receive endorsements of his callous remark, but none came. They were taking their cue from the foreman, who was glaring angrily at his associate.

'You got something against wire?' asked Fred Onslow.

'Every cattleman has something against all fences. The beeves have to feed where the grass is growing. It ain't right to stop them reaching it and that fence won't be standing much longer.'

'That is the property of the Riddle family,' the sheriff told him. 'I'll arrest any man who damages it.'

'That's hot air, Sheriff. It won't frighten Mr Benton.'

'I've told you to be quiet, Chas. I'll do the talking here,' snapped Rod Westerway. Having put Chas Tulley in his place he then addressed Sheriff Onslow. 'The boy's right though, and you know it. The boss's cows graze on this land and we can't have them damaged by that wire.'

'You tell Mr Benton what I said. And tell him one other thing: the man who was killed was unarmed. That makes it murder and I intend to hang the guilty party.'

'Perhaps you should tell him yourself.'

'You might be right at that. I'll pay him a visit tomorrow.'

'I'll tell him.' Rod Westerway pulled on the reins, turned his horse and galloped down to the river. He rode across it, the others close on his heels.

Dan and Fred watched them until they were gone from sight, at which point Dan slipped the pistol he'd been holding in his hand back into its holster.

'How long have you been holding that?' asked the sheriff.

'All the time. I turned square on so they wouldn't see me remove it from the holster. If it had come to a gunfight I would have needed every advantage I could get. I'm accurate with a gun but not fast.'

'You're a tricky one.'

'Also observant. There's a hundred rips and material

pulls in Tulley's jacket. They are similar to the ones in mine.' He stretched out his arms so that the sheriff could examine the damage to his clothing. 'These are the result of disentangling Ben Riddle from the barbed-wire fence.'

'As I said,' mused Fred Onslow, 'I'm in need of a deputy.'

# CHAPTER FOUR

On the ride back to Beecher Gulch Fred Onslow advised Dan to book into the Bright Star hotel, which he vouched for as being the best in town. That suited Dan because he figured that the best would also be the choice of any federal officer sent to interview him. In response to a couple of delicate enquiries Dan learned from the sheriff that no other newcomers had arrived in town since the influx of settlers who were now camped on the south meadow. This information cast worry in Dan's mind that Mark Clement had been unable to persuade the authorities to listen to his story.

'How often does the train come to Beecher Gulch,' he asked.

'Every three days in either direction, but it only stops if there is someone or something to unload, or if we flag it down. Usually the guard just throws off our bundle of mail as it slows past the ticket office.' The sheriff informed Dan that the next train going east was due the following day and the next one going west the day after.

True to his word, Fred Onslow did spring dinner for Dan that night, the surprise being that it was to share a home-cooked meal, to which invitation the sheriff would brook no protest.

'We get little fresh company,' he admitted, 'and my wife serves up a better meal than anything you can expect to get at the Bright Star.'

So, following the directions he'd been given and dressed in new duds that he'd obtained from Theo Dawlish's emporium, Dan strolled up the hill. It was a single-storey house, painted green, and Fred Onslow was watching for him on the veranda. Mrs Onslow, Annie, was a round-faced woman with bright eyes and a pleasant though reticent smile. She seemed to be endowed with an inherent nervousness, anxious for her guest's good opinion while being doubtful of her own ability to entertain in a fitting manner. Dan Freemont's complimentary remarks regarding the meal, which were made with true sincerity, merely embarrassed the sheriff's wife into a silent fluster.

Their daughter's personality, however, was cut mainly from her father's cloth. Cora Onslow owed the brightness of her eyes to her mother but the permanent glint of humour that they held to her father. Playfully, she chided Dan for attributing to her mother all the credit for the meal when she, Cora, was just as responsible, but she listened eagerly when he spoke of the meals he'd eaten in grand hotels across the continent. Cora had never been further than Cheyenne and she enjoyed Dan's description of New Orleans, Memphis and the cities of the East.

The evening passed swiftly and pleasantly and when it was time to go Fred Onslow stepped outside with his visitor.

'I have another favour to ask,' he said.

'It was a great dinner, Fred,' Dan told him, 'but I'm still not going to be your deputy.'

Fred chuckled. 'My charm must be slipping,' he said; then, more seriously, he added: 'I'm committed to going out to the Flying B tomorrow but Cora wants to drive out to the Riddle place. Normally, I wouldn't be concerned about her being alone but just at the moment with the trouble that's simmering over the settlers I'd be happier if she had an escort.'

'I wanted to be in town when the train came through. Perhaps the person I have to meet will be on it.'

'It doesn't come through until late afternoon. You won't miss it.'

Dan had to confess to himself that spending more time in the young woman's company would not be a punishment. It wasn't simply that she was young and pretty but her humour and eager mind had made him smile more than he could remember doing in a long while. Dressed plainly in a dull green dress with soft white frills at the neck and cuffs, she was unlike any woman he'd been with for a long time. There was a naturalness to her appearance and behaviour that had long been stripped from the elegant and painted ladies who inhabited the normal sphere of his existence. Just at that moment, the door opened and Cora stepped out on to the porch.

'Oh! you're still here,' she began. 'Mother and I were wondering if you'd like to join us on Saturday? There's going to be a raising-bee at the Keogh place.'

'A raising-bee?'

'The Keoghs are putting up a barn. Everyone goes along to help. The men work and the women prepare food and at the end of the day there's music and dancing.'

Politely, Dan explained that he might have left Beecher Gulch before then, news that clearly disappointed Cora.

'However,' Dan continued, 'I understand from your father that you intend to visit Mrs Riddle in the morning and I wondered if I could accompany you. I don't know much about farming but perhaps I'll be of some assistance.'

Dan's mount had covered a lot of territory during the previous few days so Dan left it stabled behind the hotel and drove the buggy with Cora at his side. Her father accompanied them as far as the ford, two miles outside town, where he crossed the river and headed east to the Flying B. The day was warm and Dan and Cora were as relaxed in each other's company as they had been the night before.

Sarah Riddle was not in the sod house when they drew to a halt outside the door. Nor was she in the lean-to where the implements, seed and produce were stored, nor the timber shed that housed the horse and two-seat buggy. Dan scanned the horizon, his eyes following the line of the wire fence which Ben Riddle had been erecting when he was killed. At the full extent of his view, where the land rose to a low ridge, he saw the widow. Her head was uncovered and her long hair was stretched behind her by the warm breeze. Leaving Cora, he walked up the meadow with determined stride. As he approached he removed his hat and stood with it in his hand until Mrs Riddle turned her head to look at him.

'You're the deputy,' she said.

'I was with the sheriff yesterday. Yes ma'am.'

She turned again to look over the falling land. Corn was knee high on a section close at hand and there were two other patches off to the right where various vegetables grew.

'It wasn't easy,' she said, her voice soft so that Dan wasn't sure whether she was addressing him or her thoughts had slipped out through her mouth. 'Ploughing that little patch in time to plant the seeds before the ground became rock hard with frost.'

She turned to face him again. 'Winter comes here early. We didn't know that. Turned out that there were a lot of things we didn't know about the weather here and probably we had a lot still to learn. But we got that done last year and now our first crop is growing. You should have seen Ben's face when the first stalks appeared. I've seen men three parts of the way down a jug with less silly grins on their face. He was so proud to have a crop in his first year.

'Over there,' she said, pointing to a section further down the slope, 'he ploughed all that in the spring. Him, me and the horse. The seed is ready for planting. Next year the yield will be greater.' Her steady grey eyes fixed on the distant patch, her mouth firm and her chin lifted to reflect her husband's pride. 'I'd like him buried here,' she said, 'where he can look down on his achievement.'

Dan studied the woman; her final words had taken him by surprise.

'The townspeople expect him to be buried in their cemetery. People are coming out to help you pack your belongings and take you into town. Cora Onslow, the sheriff's daughter came with me this morning to offer her help.'

'Pack? I'm not going anywhere.'

'You mean to stay here? Alone?'

'This was what Ben and I wanted – land of our own, room to fling out our arms in the morning and not disturb our neighbours.'

The irony of Sarah Riddle's last remark wasn't lost on Dan; it was probably their neighbours who killed her husband.

'Will you bring Ben's body out here for me?' she asked.

'If that's what you want, but I'd urge you to consider your position. There's trouble here. The cattlemen who don't want any settlers are threatening more violence. The law might not be able to prevent it. You wouldn't be safe, Mrs Riddle.' In his mind he was picturing a raid by cowboys who would not only ride through the crop fields but over Ben Riddle's grave, a desecration that could be more damaging to her spirit than the loss of produce to her pocket.

But Sarah's decision was made. When she spoke it wasn't with anger or false bravery. She was serene, her face turned into the breeze so that her lifted head showed a profile of stateliness from the high intelligent brow to the fragile line of her slender neck. She presented an aura of beauty such as Dan had never seen before.

'Ben wouldn't leave if I'd been killed,' she said. ' He would resist any effort to deprive him of this land. I can be no different.'

Dan had nothing but admiration for the widow's stance and her declaration that she wouldn't be chased from the land, but he hoped that when the initial shock of her husband's death had passed away, or by heeding the sympathetic counsel of Fred Onslow or some other town stalwart, she would reconsider her decision. In the future, greedy, ruthless men would not be her only enemy, nature itself would be her greatest foe. Not only was the land difficult to turn but the summers brought blistering heat and the winters were long and bitterly cold. Then there was prairie fever, despairing loneliness as a result of days or weeks without human company, a condition responsible for many settlers being robbed of their sanity.

But this wasn't the time to try to convince her that

she should quit this section of land and by the time she was more susceptible to persuasion he expected to be well clear of the territory. For now she was mourning her husband, so he left the girls alone to talk, threw a saddle over the Riddles's work horse and rode the fence line down towards the river.

Ever since the previous day's confrontation with Rod Westerway there had been uneasiness in Dan's mind about Sarah Riddle's safety. Now, following her declared intention to remain on the isolated strip of land, that uneasiness had increased. His object as he rode east was to inspect the wire, to make sure that Carl Benton's men hadn't returned to pull the stakes from the ground.

Topping the ridge of land that sloped down to the riverside trail he'd ridden yesterday, Dan was confronted with a scene that confirmed his worst expectation. Ugly little twists and coils of barbed wire that had been cut away from the posts were scattered about on the ground, and the posts themselves had been uprooted and cast aside. A stretch of fence about thirty yards long had been destroyed in this manner and the men who had done it were still at work. Dan recognized them as Carl Benton's men from the previous day.

One of the men was afoot, cutting the strands of wire and pushing them aside with his gloved hands so that they didn't spring back to rip his flesh or clothing. The other man was astride a grey horse. He'd thrown his lasso over the next post, waiting to pull it out of the ground when his companion had cut free the bottom strand. The mounted man was Chas Tulley and his voice carried up the hill to the watching Dan. The words were indistinct but it was clear that the young man was enjoying his destructive task.

Being somewhat to the rear of the fence-busters, Dan Freemont had not yet been spotted by them. For a moment he continued to observe, then he nudged the horse forward, knowing he had only one course of action. He was a reluctant gunman but in this instance he could discern no alternative. He drew the Colt from the holster on his hip and fired. The bullet passed the grey's nose and struck the post around which Tulley's rope had been thrown. The horse shied, stepped backwards and, with a nervous whinny, reared high.

Tulley, surprised by both the gunshot and the movement of the horse, released his hold on his lasso and gripped the reins in order to regain control of the animal under him. However, his reactions were sharp and he was halfway to drawing his gun when the voice behind him commanded otherwise.

'From this distance I can't miss,' shouted Dan Freemont. He wasn't sure if he was telling the truth but his commanding tone meant that the other two men weren't prepared to doubt him. 'You are both under arrest,' he announced. 'You,' he said to the man on the ground, 'throw aside those cutters, then with your left hand unbuckle your gunbelt and let it fall.' From the corner of his eye Dan watched Chas Tulley; he could see the cowboy's right hand twitch as though he were preparing to take a chance, wondering if he could draw and fire while Dan's concentration was centred on Sim Taylor. To remove any doubt Dan spoke.

'I'll blow you out of the saddle if your hand moves any closer to that six-shooter.'

Chas Tulley froze, glaring at Dan with hatred because his impotence was being witnessed by Sim Taylor. After Sim had disarmed himself it was Tulley's turn to unbuckle his belt. In addition, Dan kept his pistol pointed at the cowboy's belly while he tossed aside the rifle from the scabbard under his right leg. Under the threat of Dan's gun, Sim mounted his horse, but not before his rifle, too, was thrown on to the dust of the Riddles's settlement.

Dan pointed across the river. 'Now ride,' he commanded.

'That's not the way to town,' Sim Taylor declared.

'We're going to the Flying B first.'

The curiosity of Carl Benton's men turned to amusement when Dan told them that he meant to arrest the rancher too, if he had instructed them to destroy the fence. The real reason was that he hoped to find Sheriff Onslow at the Flying B. The real lawman would determine how to proceed against the fence-cutting criminals.

Chas Tulley poured scorn on Dan as they rode, assuring him that Carl Benton would have him stripped, hogtied and sent back to Beecher Gulch over his saddle. Sim Taylor, on the other hand, said very little. He was wary of the man who had caught them red-handed and arrested them. Dan commanded with a confidence that made Sim wonder if he was a special officer brought in by the sheriff to keep order.

Although he wasn't showing any anxiety Dan's main concern was that Sheriff Onslow had already quit the Flying B, which could mean that he was indeed riding into trouble. However, his current route joined the trail to Beecher Gulch, so he anticipated intercepting the lawman along the way. To increase the chance of the sheriff still being at the ranch when they arrived, he insisted upon maintaining a good speed as his two prisoners led the way across the dry land to Carl Benton's ranch.

The grin that Chas Tulley flashed at a couple of ranch hands as they rode into the ranch yard quickly disappeared when he recognized the man who accompanied his boss on the ranch house veranda. Sheriff Onslow had been on the point of leaving when the threesome arrived, and when he identified Dan as the third rider his interest was aroused. The speed at which they'd entered the compound had also grabbed the attention of one or two of the men in the yard and, inquisitiveness being the nature of most cowboys, they wandered towards the porch to learn the news. Sheriff Onslow was first to speak, voicing his surprise at Dan's presence.

'Thought you were staying with my daughter at Mrs Riddle's place.'

'That was the plan until I caught these two pulling down her limit fence.'

Instantly Fred Onslow challenged Carl Benton. 'Is this your doing? Were they acting on your orders?'

Jacketless, the bull strength of Carl Benton was clear to see. Towering over the sheriff, his shoulders were wide and his neck thick. His head was big, its size emphasized by the sparseness of his trimmed ginger hair, and the redness of his complexion lent him a permanent look of anger. His green eyes flashed towards Chas Tulley and for a moment he seemed prepared to deny that they were any part of his operation. Eventually, with a shrug, he conceded that they were part of his crew.

'Perhaps the boys misunderstood me; they've acted hastily,' he told Fred Onslow. 'My views on fences are well enough known and now that that stretch is vacant again I suppose removing the fence seemed the best thing to do to prevent injury to my herd.'

'This is the kind of behaviour I came here to warn you against, Benton,' the sheriff replied. 'I don't intend to stand by while a range war develops. Settlers are here at the behest of the government. They have a legal right to the land they settle on and if they want to build fences then that's all right, too. They are entitled to the protection of the law and that's what they'll get while I'm sheriff around here.

'Now I told that galoot yesterday that I'd arrest anyone who caused damage to that fence and that's what I'll do. Those two are coming to Beecher Gulch with me and they'll stay in jail until I can get a judge to try them.'

'Wait a minute, Sheriff,' Benton expostulated, 'I need those men. This is a busy time. There's work to be done.'

'I can't help that. They broke the law. They'll stay locked up until a judge gets to town.'

It was clear that neither Chas Tulley nor Sim Taylor relished the prospect of jail and they appealed to their boss for help.

'What about bail?' asked Carl Benton. Fred Onslow rubbed his jaw thoughtfully.

'How much damage did these men do?' he asked Dan Freemont.

'About a hundred feet of fence destroyed, poles uprooted and wire cut away.'

'Mrs Riddle, I suppose, will have to pay someone to re-erect that fence and the materials will have to be replaced. Tell you what, Mr Benton, I'll set bail at a hundred dollars a man plus another hundred to cover the damage they've done. You give me three hundred dollars and a promise that these men will be surrendered to my office when the judge gets to town and I'll leave them in your care.'

It was a reluctant Carl Benton who handed a bundle of greenbacks to the sheriff, 300 dollars being a price well in excess of Tulley's and Taylor's worth as cowpushers, but if matters came to a head, if he was to stop the settlement of the open range and provide free pasture for his herd, then they would be no good to him in prison. Despite the sheriff's words, he meant to scare every settler out of the territory.

As he mounted his horse, however, Fred Onslow threw a suggestion in the ranch owner's direction.

'At the moment I can't prove that you or any of your men had a hand in the murder of Ben Riddle, and perhaps I never will, but if you want that land you are going to have to buy it.'

'Buy it? It's free land.'

'It was free land until the Riddles began to work it. Now it's that woman's property. You make her a good offer because it's cost her husband's life.'

'Any offer should be made through the sheriff's office. Mrs Riddle's place is off limits to you and your men,' Dan Freemont added.

'Don't get too uppity, Deputy,' Chas Tulley warned Dan, 'I won't always be without a gun.'

'Are you threatening an officer of the law?' Fred Onslow's voice was rich with threat. 'Bail or not, you'll be spending time in the town jail if you do that again.'

'Where are your guns?' asked Carl Benton.

'On Riddle's land.'

'I'll throw them across the river for you,' Dan told him. 'Perhaps some of them will make it to the far bank.'

# CHAPTER FIVE

'I guess you're surprised that I didn't take those two into custody?'

Since leaving the Flying B they'd ridden almost a mile towards the river without speaking, but Dan's silence owed more to concern for Sarah Riddle's safety than curiosity about his companion's decision. Although he had little evidence on which to base his assessment, Dan judged Fred Onslow to be a fair-minded man who was more than competent as a peace officer. Dan had taken the fence-busters to the Flying B because he needed the sheriff to decide the appropriate action, so he had no cause to criticize the other's ruling.

'They'll still be tried,' Dan replied, 'and you've already fined them for damages. I don't suppose a circuit judge will achieve much more.'

Sheriff Onslow chuckled. 'Are you sure you don't want a job as my deputy? You're thinking like one – and behaving like one, too. And,' he added, 'arresting those boys has Benton's crew assuming you are one.'

'I was angry because they intended to ride rough-shod over Mrs Riddle's property. She wants her husband buried there and intends to stay and work the land. She needs advice, Sheriff, from someone with experience of this territory.'

'Are you suggesting me?'

'I know it's a bad time to try to convince her of anything but she needs to be persuaded quickly. Once her husband's body is buried on that strip she won't quit it.'

Fred Onslow agreed with Dan's assessment of the situation; the ceaseless labour, the loneliness and the danger to a woman alone pointed to a harsh, unrewarding existence. And the danger to Sarah Riddle, he believed, was more than a possibility.

'I had two reasons for setting bail for those back at the Flying B,' he told Dan. 'First, there is no telling when a judge will get here and I didn't want them on my hands for an indefinite period. The town has to feed them and, not having a deputy,' he lifted his eyes in Dan's direction, 'find and pay for an extra night guard.'

'Didn't take you for a miser,' Dan told him.

'When you are sheriff you have to be a little bit of everything.'

'What was your second reason for setting bail?'

'To test Carl Benton. A hundred dollars is quite a demand for a replaceable dollar-a-day cowpoke. Benton isn't exactly renowned for his generosity to the hired help, yet he barely quibbled at handing over three hundred dollars to keep those two on the ranch.'

'What do you make of that?'

'Could be a number of things but my guess is that he has a particular use for them. Chas Tulley fancies himself as a gunhand and this morning's work is proof that he's prepared to buck the law. I don't buy Benton's claim that his hands pulled down that fence without his authority, nor do I believe that he would stand bail for them if they had done so. He means to kick up trouble, I'm sure of that. He's determined to keep the range open and doesn't care who gets hurt in the process.'

'So you are on the side of the settlers?'

'I'm only on the side of the law, but men like Carl Benton have to realize that times are changing. There may be only a dribble of settlers at the moment but it won't always be like that. The railway has made this territory accessible from east and west and when word gets around about the fertility of the valleys people will come here in droves.'

He paused, wiped his hand across his lips and darted a glance at Dan as though anxious to add more but unsure of the words he wanted to say.

'In a few years,' he eventually said, 'there'll be a clamour for statehood but that will only be achieved when there are families here to raise schools and churches and when all disputes are settled by the law. Perhaps, like the Indian wars, a confrontation will be required before that day can be realized. Those cattle-men who have flourished despite Indian raids, rustlers and violent nature believe that every inch of land on which their cattle have grazed belongs to them.

'But the United States of America own the land and they want to see it improved and developed. To a simple man like me, a clash seems inevitable.'

'And you stand in the middle.'

'I stand where I want to stand. I might be looking far into the future and it might never be realized in my lifetime, but for Cora and her children statehood would signify that Wyoming was a settled and prospering territory. To achieve that, however, we have to prove ourselves capable of government and maintaining law and order.'

To Dan's belief, no man had ever before disclosed to him such personal thoughts. He didn't understand why Fred Onslow had done so now, they being acquaintances of less than a couple of days, yet from the first moment the sheriff's affability and friendliness had been apparent. Dan couldn't fire up a response but that was due to the fact that talk of government had raised afresh in his mind the need to get back to town for the arrival of the eastbound train.

Another buggy stood alongside Cora Onslow's when they got to Sarah Riddle's house. It had brought the doctor and his wife, and Sarah's firmly set expression made it clear that she had repeated to them her intention of not removing to town. The doctor, an ageing, stooped man called Pope, came outside to greet them and inform the sheriff of the bereaved woman's decision.

'I think she's making a mistake, Fred,' the doctor

told him, 'but hopefully she will reconsider after a few days on her own.'

A few moments later, joined by his wife, the doctor drove his buggy back towards Beecher Gulch.

Sheriff Onslow handed over the hundred dollars for damages to Sarah Riddle. It took only an instant for her to make the leap from damage to the fence to the murder of her husband.

'Is that why Ben was murdered? Because he put up a fence?'

Sheriff Onslow tried to be diplomatic. 'We don't know who killed him yet. Until we do we can't be sure of the reason for it.'

Sarah Riddle scoffed at the answer. 'You think there's room for doubt?'

'There's no proof. I can't arrest anyone until there is.'

'Carl Benton has made more than one threat against the settlers,' she said.

'I know, and it is for that reason that everyone would prefer you to go into town.'

'You think he'll come after me next? You think he'll kill a woman but you won't arrest him?'

Fred Onslow gave an embarrassed shrug. He was counting on Carl Benton to make an offer for Sarah Riddle's land but there was no guarantee that he would. During his visit to the Flying B, Fred had made it clear that Benton and his crew were the prime suspects for the murder and he hoped that that and the warning to stay on their own side of the river was enough to prevent any molestation of the widow.

'What about you, Deputy?' she asked Dan.

'I told you my thoughts earlier. Staying here alone won't be easy.'

'Does that mean you are breaking your promise? That you won't bring my husband's body out here to be buried?'

'No, I won't break my promise. If that is still what you want then I'll do it and dig the grave for you. I'm just asking you to hold off for a few days, give yourself a little time to think it all through.'

'I've thought about it. I've decided. I want him buried tomorrow.'

Shortly after that they left Sarah Riddle alone and returned to Beecher Gulch.

The thick smoke had been visible for several minutes, the distant black dot had grown to become the front of the locomotive's iron boiler and the low rumble that had announced its approach was now topped by a piercing whistle of steam as it reached the town's boundary. The train slowed but by the time it was halfway along the platform it was clear that it wouldn't be stopping. From the caboose the guard threw two mailbags and raised a hand in greeting to the stationmaster. Then he closed the door and the eastbound train picked up speed and diminished into the distance.

Although it had always seemed more likely to Dan that anyone sent from the US marshal's office would come from the East, he was still disappointed that another day was about to pass without contact. He was in limbo, waiting, unable to influence proceedings in any way. He toyed with the idea of sending a telegraph message to Mark Clement. He didn't have to put his full name to it; the fact that it had been sent from Beecher Gulch would be signature enough. His plan, however, was postponed when a figure that had been leaning at the corner of the ticket building stepped forward and addressed him.

'Perhaps you'll have better luck tomorrow.'

'Is my business of such interest to you?' he asked the sheriff.

Fred Onslow chuckled. 'You shouldn't attach so much importance to yourself. I usually hang around the station when a train comes in. Keeps me up to date with the comings and goings. Can't be too careful. Wouldn't want the town to be a regular stopping-off place for criminals.'

Dan thought he detected a hidden message in the sheriff's tone but brushed his suspicion aside, attributing it to his own edginess and Sheriff Onslow's humour.

'I guess it means that you're free to take Ben Riddle's body out to his widow's place and help bury him.'

'I reckon so.'

'That still your intention?'

'I said I would do it so I don't have a choice.'

'Even though you think it's the wrong thing to do?'

'Look, Sheriff, I'm not going to be around this town much longer and my involvement with your local problem will end when I go. Until then I'm content to assist Mrs Riddle. I have no power to persuade her to do anything she doesn't want to do and I wouldn't if I could. If she chooses to remain here then she has a struggle ahead of her. She's aware of that and is prepared to fight. There isn't anything more that I can do about it.'

'What about Carl Benton's offer to buy the land?'

'What about it? He hasn't made an offer and, frankly, I'll be surprised if he does. And I don't suppose Mrs Riddle will accept an offer from him. She, like you and me, knows that he is responsible for the death of her husband. Burying her husband on that land is a mark of her determination to stay. It might quicken the confrontation that is brewing. Mrs Riddle quitting her land won't prevent it.'

When they parted Dan walked down to Sepp Lucas's funeral parlour and made arrangements to collect Ben Riddle's body early next morning. On learning that the burial was a private affair the undertaker offered Dan the services of his assistant, who would help to dig the grave and get the body into the ground.

'He's in a box,' Sepp Lucas said. 'It'll take at least two of you.' After Dan's acceptance he offered more advice. 'Best not to let the widow see her husband. Those bullets to the head made a mess of his face. I've done all I'm capable of doing to improve the damage but she still shouldn't have to see him like that.'

With the prospect of a busy day ahead Dan returned to the Bright Star and an evening meal in the dining room. Afterwards, tempted by the balmy night, he went out on to the front veranda but he lingered there only a few moments. The heavy pounding of a bar-room piano lured him along the street to the building that had no other name than Saloon. It was more than a week since Dan had last held a handful of cards, which was the longest abstinence he could recall. So when he pushed aside the batwing doors his first scan of the room was to find a table where a game of poker was in progress.

It was a deep room with the long bar on the left stretching down almost to the furthest point. It had no gallery, no upstairs rooms, but there was a door behind the bar that led, presumably, to a store room, and another door at the bottom end of the room that provided access to a couple of rooms which were regularly pressed into service by two or three of the town's professional ladies.

Apart from the man behind the bar and the pianist, all the other men had been drawn towards a table against the right-hand wall. Abandoned cards and drinks at other tables testified to the fact that this was an impromptu meeting. More than two dozen men surrounded the table in haphazard fashion; some had simply turned their chairs in that direction while the remainder were standing in the gaps between tables or leaning against the wall where they could be closer to the speaker. Those at that central table had remained in their seats, and from there, above the general murmur of the crowd, an Irish brogue angrily commanded the pianist to cease playing. At the same moment the batwing doors clattered to announce Dan Freemont's entrance and, momentarily, silence descended on the room.

'Drink somewhere else, mister,' called one of the group, but his order was quickly challenged.

'No, wait, that's the guy who brought in Ben's body. Let's get some facts from him.'

It was clear from their apparel that the men in the room were not cowherders. There was no evidence of boots, spurs or Stetsons, nor did anyone wear a gunbelt, instead the men wore rough woollen trousers or bib-fronted denims over faded cotton shirts that in many instances were collarless. Some men wore jackets but all were hatless. They were farmers and settlers, some of whom were in town to collect provisions, others had wandered into the saloon from the tent camp on the outskirts.

For a brief second Dan considered taking heed of the first speaker. He could get a glass of whiskey in the Bright Star. As he'd recently remarked to Sheriff Onslow, the events taking place in Beecher Gulch weren't his concern: he'd be gone soon enough. But he'd also said that he was prepared to help Sarah Riddle and it was clear that the congregation before him had known her husband. Perhaps he would be able to garner some assistance for her when they learned that she intended to stay and work the land. He walked towards the group.

The Irishman was called Shaughnessey and, like so many of his race whom Dan had encountered, he sounded angry with every word he uttered.

'Who are you? What are you doing here?'

Dan supplied the name Dan Bayles and told them that he had business in town but would soon be moving on.

'Mrs Riddle has asked me to bury her husband on their land tomorrow. After that I mean to finish the fence her husband had begun stringing. It needs to be completed to protect her property. I haven't done much in the way of farming so I'd be grateful for any help I can get.'

There were a few mumbles that defied interpretation but Tommy Keogh, who had been the main voice before Dan's entrance, was the one who latched on to the fact that Sarah Riddle was staying on her property.

'She believes that Ben wouldn't have quit if she'd been the one killed, so she won't quit either.'

'That's my position, too,' roared Shaughnessey. 'I didn't cross an ocean just to turn tail because somebody doesn't like my face.'

'Nobody likes your face, Sam,' said a wag.

It brought a brief moment of mirth to the gathering but Shaughnessey was not to be deterred from his declamation.

'According to Sheriff Onslow there isn't any proof that Carl Benton killed Ben, but who else would do it and wrap him up in that blasted wire? Benton vowed to kill any man who stopped his cattle gaining access to grazing land or water and that's what he's done. We can't let him get away with it or he'll attack each of us.'

'What are you suggesting?' demanded Tommy Keogh. 'That we take the law in our own hands and attack him? We aren't gunfighters. We can't risk our lives when we have families to protect.'

'That's the point, Tommy. We'll protect them better if we drive Benton out of the territory.'

'You're talking about range war,' interjected Dan, 'which is the very thing that Sheriff Onslow is trying to avoid. In the short term you won't win. Carl Benton can afford to bring in an army of guns and destroy all of you. It has happened in other parts of cattle country. You have to beat him with the law. Sheriff Onslow is a good man. Give him time to prove Benton's guilt.'

'I agree,' said Tommy Keogh.

Sam Shaughnessey snapped at his fellow home-steader. 'It's a mistake to think you won't be troubled by Benton just because your farm is upriver. Benton's the kind of man who won't be satisfied until he has every-thing. Doing nothing won't appease him.'

The sound of a bell being rung brought Dan and many another resident of Beecher Gulch from their slumber in the dark morning hours of the following day. Over the dull monotonous clang someone was yelling and the combination of sounds triggered a sense of alarm in all who heard it.

'*Fire!*'

Dan was pulling on his shirt as he left his hotel room and made for the street in company with several other grim-faced men. There wasn't a moment to lose: fire could destroy a town. Flames from one timber frame would pass swiftly to another so that a whole street could be an inferno in a matter of minutes. Fighting fires was the civic duty of everyone in town.

On the street, however, there seemed to be a momentary pause. The expected sight of a burning building was absent, there was no evidence of flames or smoke rising into the black sky. All eyes turned to the man who had raised the alarm, Zach Hartnell, who extended his arm to point down the street.

'The tents,' he explained, 'the tent camp is on fire,'

As everyone's gaze was directed south a red glow that coloured the darkness behind the last of the town's buildings could be seen. Instantly each man knew that the distance to the tents was too great to organize a bucket chain from the pump and that their only hope of saving the tents was by fetching water from the river. They ran, each man with a bucket snatched from a collection outside the emporium, but as they sprinted past the blacksmith's forge they knew that they faced a hopeless task.

Every tent, it seemed, was aflame. Silhouettes flickered here and there among the mass of burning material. People were shouting, running towards their would-be rescuers, stopping, yelling names of family and friends lost in the inferno. Wild-eyed children clung to the coats of parents whose dream of a new life was being cremated before their eyes.

The townspeople did all they could, running with buckets of water from the nearby river to quench the blaze, but it was a battle they were always going to lose. Throughout the night the men continued in their struggle to put out the fire while the womenfolk tended to the needs of the evacuees. The saloon was pressed into service as a gathering point and hospital so that families could be counted and injuries attended to. Two people were missing: a mother and her son. Their charred remains would not be found until the sun came up.

# CHAPTER SIX

In common with every other man in Beecher Gulch, Dan Freemont worked tirelessly to quell the fire. He carried water from the river until the fire marshals were forced to concede that the blaze was beyond control. Then, as a precaution against a shift in wind direction, he joined a team of men digging a ditch in the meadow to contain the spread of flames.

With the coming of dawn's light the fire began to abate and the total destruction of the camp was apparent to all. Every tent and its contents had been destroyed; all that remained were smouldering piles among the ankle-deep black ash, and rising smoke which carried with it the searing smell of disaster. By this time it was clear that the risk of the fire spreading to the town buildings no longer existed and the fire marshals, Zach Hartnell and Theo Dawlish, began to release teams of men from duty.

When Dan's turn to stand down arrived he made his way to the Bright Star where breakfast was available for every firefighter. On the way he passed the saloon where Cora Onslow was attending to a handful of evacuated children. They exchanged a look but it was no time for pleasantries and he continued down the street to the hotel. Fred Onslow sat beside him but there was little conversation, both men were grimy, coughing and engaged in their own thoughts.

If, by daylight, the inhabitants of Beecher Gulch had anything for which to be grateful it was the fact that the site of the camp had been sufficiently removed from the town to keep the inferno isolated, and that the breeze had been blowing in the wrong direction to make airborne sparks a danger to the timber buildings. None the less, if the citizens weren't troubled by the smoke that continued to arise from the remaining embers, the gloom of the disaster still shrouded their morning. Soot-stained weary men and women gossiped in groups or lingered on the boardwalks, as though their recent labours had sucked every vestige of energy from their muscles and every purpose from their life. No haste could be discerned in their actions: every man looked as forlorn as his neighbour.

The despondency of the townsfolk, however, was overshadowed by the utter despair of those who had fled in the night from the raging fire. Some wandered among the still smouldering remains, heads bowed as, in abject despair, with faces as grey as the overhead smoke, they scuffed the ground, although it was clear that they had no expectation of finding any of their belongings intact.

Accompanied by Hal Granger, Sepp Lucas's assistant, and with the coffin on the flat boards behind,

Dan drove Ben Riddle's wagon slowly past the rased site. Other people's misfortune had never troubled him before: not for a moment had he considered the consequences of a fellow player losing a walletful of money. He had always attended to his own problems and expected other people to do likewise, but he couldn't ignore the depth of misery etched on the faces of those hopelessly searching through the debris of their possessions.

He wondered how many dreams had been ended by this tragic accident. Whatever expectations had brought them West, whatever troubles they might have been prepared to face, the instant loss of all their possessions was a trial that few would be able to overcome.

Owning land had never been Dan's dream. Working from sunup to sunset in conditions produced by the whim of the weather was, in his opinion, work fit only for those who had no other talent. His tastes were more civilized and when he bought property it would have a butler to open the door. Never before had he seen men whose faces so betrayed a broken spirit, whose movements were without significance and for whom life had become devoid of meaning. He clicked the reins at the walking horse and raised it to a trot.

The wagon had been more than a mile away when Sarah Riddle first recognized it, and she had waited at the door until it halted in her yard. She wore a blue dress with a buttoned bodice and Dan guessed that it was the one her husband had liked to see her in. Her fair hair was piled on her head and held together at the back with a tortoiseshell fastener. She greeted them with little more than a nod, then, against Dan's advice, insisted that the lid of the coffin be raised so that she could take a final look at her husband.

True to his word, Sepp Lucas had undertaken some reconstruction of the corpse's features but the damage done by the three head shots remained ugly. One bullet had gone into Ben's forehead at such an angle that, on exit, it had lifted away a section of his skull. A second bullet had struck him at the bridge of his nose so that he appeared to have a third eye, and the third had blown away part of his left cheek.

'Sepp took eight slugs out of his body,' Hal Granger informed Dan and Sarah Riddle, 'and the other scars were caused by the barbed wire. It wasn't easy getting it off.'

Dan thought the man's bluntness was unnecessary, but the widow betrayed no emotion. She turned away and headed up to the rise of land where she wanted Ben to be buried. When they'd refixed the lid Dan and Hal drove up to join her. After digging the grave, they put the coffin in the ground.

No words were spoken over Ben Riddle; his widow stood alone, keeping her thoughts and memories to herself. There were no tears to express sorrow or loss and if she was planning or praying for vengeance she kept it well disguised. When she faced the men to indicate that they could finish the job, it seemed to Dan that her resolve to stay had been strengthened. Her tight-lipped expression added determination to the serenity of her mien. She walked back down to the sod house while Dan and Hal filled in the grave.

Because the wagon and horse belonged to Sarah Riddle, Hal and Dan had brought their own horses for the return journey. Hal departed as soon as the task was completed but Dan wanted to reassure himself before returning to town that no more damage had been done to the property. First, however, he accepted a mug of coffee from the young widow. While they drank he told her about the fire and the consequent probability that no one in Beecher Gulch would have the time to help her.

'I have to return to town now,' he told her, 'and I'll be quitting this territory soon, but if I'm still here tomorrow I'll ride out and do what I can to fix up your damaged fence. Perhaps in a week or two you'll be able to hire someone to complete it for you.'

'I'll manage,' she told him, but he wasn't sure he believed her.

As he climbed into the saddle she spoke. 'Deputy,' she said, 'I don't know your name.'

'It's Dan,' he told her. 'Dan Bayles.'

He rode down to the riverside trail. No more damage had been inflicted on the fence but Dan climbed down to inspect the poles that had been uprooted. For a moment the prospect of tackling the job on his own seemed ridiculous: he didn't know the first thing about erecting a fence. Sarah Riddle's face, however, came to his mind and he recalled the determination he'd seen in her eyes. She was proud, he realized, and intended to work the land she owned with or without help from

anyone in Beecher Gulch. If she had that determination, he resolved, then he wouldn't fail her. He would
return in the morning and reset the posts.

During Dan's absence a town meeting had been
convened to consider the plight of the distressed
settlers. It had been held in the largest public room of
the Bright Star because in one corner it boasted a small
stage from which the town committee could address
the gathering. Fred Onslow had stood there alongside
Zach Hartnell and Theo Dawlish, the last-named
acting as chairman. Of the twenty families, eight had
decided to quit the territory. Already unnerved by
the death of Ben Riddle and aware of the prospect
of violence that it trumpeted, the total loss of their
possessions provided an acceptable reason to return
East. No-one criticized them for choosing to leave; the
decision to stay or go was one that each family had to
make for itself, but those who had decided otherwise
were vociferous in their reasons for staying.

'We came out here to claim land of our own.
We wouldn't own anything if we'd stayed back in
Pennsylvania,' said one.

'Nor I in Ohio,' chimed in another. 'There's nothing
there for us to go back to.'

'Didn't think we were moving to paradise, that there
wouldn't be problems of one kind or another to face,'
insisted a third.

'We'd like to stay,' explained a fourth speaker, 'but
everything we had has been destroyed. We're broke.

We can afford neither the train fare out of here nor the replacement of the tools and equipment we've lost. We can't even afford shelter for our children tonight.'

Theo Dawlish put everyone's mind at rest regarding their immediate future.

'The town committee has agreed to release funds from our treasury to ensure that no one is without food or shelter. For those who are staying to take up their land grants we'll provide tents, clothing and food while you remain within the town's boundaries. We'll furnish the cost of rail travel to those who mean to return East. Mr Pollard at the bank will give advice to anyone who has access to funds outside Wyoming.'

'We're not a rich town,' Zach Hartnell raised his voice above the conversation of those gathered before them, 'and we aren't demanding repayment of any money, but we won't refuse any future contribution to the town's exchequer.' Zach had been opposed to his friend's carte blanche approach to the needs of the homeless settlers and thought it proper to illuminate the fact that other aspects of the town's development would suffer because funds were being diverted to this emergency cause.

Theo Dawlish listened to Zach with an understanding that was seasoned with a dash of exasperation. Despite his words, the blacksmith wasn't unsympathetic to the plight of the settlers, indeed it was he who had first voiced the necessity of giving them support in their time of need, but releasing money from the town's small treasury meant a delay to the establishment of a school: his prime desire. Theo had extracted a promise from Zach that he wouldn't press for repayment of the loan, but the big man had been unable to resist the opportunity to ask for future donations.

'Tents can be collected at my store,' Theo told those present as he brought the meeting to a close.

When Dan returned to Beecher Gulch several tents had already been erected but the new site was at the other end of town, across the railway track, where a series of mounds provided a break against prairie winds. As he awaited the arrival of the westbound train he was joined by the sheriff. Together they watched the men and women at work 200 yards distant.

'What caused the fire?' Dan asked Fred Onslow.

'Don't know. Someone said it had started in one of the back tents but someone else sited in the middle said that a tent close to him was ablaze when he heard the first alarm. Nobody has admitted responsibility. We just don't know.'

The westbound train whistled as it pulled its three carriages and caboose into town. It slowed, blew steam and stopped with a series of clanks and jerks. It hadn't been flagged down by the stationmaster, which meant that Beecher Gulch was someone's destination. Dan was convinced that his wait was over; he was sure that a US marshal was about to alight from the train. He walked towards the carriages,

From the far end, the last carriage, there was a clamour of excitement. Suddenly, men were jumping down on to the platform, laughing, slapping each other on the shoulder and looking around at the miles upon miles of open space. Then they were reaching up, grabbing bundles and cases and stacking them on the ground. Finally came the women and children who, in general, displayed the same excitement as their menfolk.

Fred Onslow estimated forty in the group. 'A dozen, perhaps fifteen families,' he muttered to Dan. 'We've had no word to say they were coming. It's a bad time. We'd hoped the others would have moved away from town before any more arrived.' He grunted. 'Nothing we can do about it.'

Dan's attention had been diverted from the clamour of the excited settlers because he'd caught sight of some movement at the rear of the middle carriage. Before he could follow up his interest a voice from behind addressed the sheriff.

'More families,' said Rod Westerway, the Flying B's foreman. 'This won't please Mr Benton.'

'Mr Benton's pleasures aren't my concern just so long as they don't break any laws,' Onslow replied

'Do you want me to tell him that?'

'He already knows, but you can tell him to keep Tulley and Taylor close to the ranch. I had a telegraph message from St Louis. A judge will be here in a day or two.'

From the boarding plate of the nearest carriage voices were raised.

'Sheriff. Sheriff.' The guard was descending the steps carrying a small travelling trunk. In his wake, dressed in a green travelling-coat and wearing a matching hat with a long, black plume, was a tall elegant redhead.

'Sheriff,' called the guard again, 'you need to lock this woman in your jail.'

'What for?' These words spoken by the redhead, her face showing both surprise and affront at such a suggestion.

The charge was supplied by another woman who now stood at the rear door of the carriage. She was middle-aged and wore that expression of righteousness that is reserved for those whose life holds no other pleasure than the prevention of it in others.

'She's a whore who shouldn't be allowed to travel with decent people.'

'I am no such thing,' returned the redhead. 'Your husband smiled to see if he was still able to. It's probably the first time he's done it since he married you.'

The woman gasped with shock but quickly regained the will to attack again. However, the guard intervened and ushered her back into the carriage. When she was safely inside he closed the door and stepped down again. Before hurrying to the back of the train to assure himself that the disembarkation of the other group was without mishap, he shot some parting words at the sheriff.

'She was gambling,' he said. 'That's why I'm putting her off the train. There'd be trouble if she stayed on to the next town.'

'Gambling?' repeated Fred Onslow.

'Isn't that what everyone does on trains?' she asked.

'Were you winning?'

'That was the reason for playing.'

'Did you take money from her husband?'

'Just a few hundred.'

'Well, we don't lock up whores in this town, nor gamblers if they don't cause trouble.'

Rod Westerway spoke. 'That must be a disappointment for the deputy here. He was ready to volunteer for night duty.'

Dan had been only half-listening to the proceedings. He was scanning the platform to see if anyone else had descended from the train. When no one had left the third carriage he had fixed his attention to the new arrivals at the far end of the platform, studying to see if there was someone among them who did not belong to the group. There wasn't, and the next day there was no train due in either direction. Yet, disappointed as he was by the non-show of a US marshal, he consoled himself with the thought that he would be able to spend the next day repairing the damaged fence on Sarah Riddle's land. He couldn't understand why he was so pleased by the prospect of work which was so foreign to his nature.

'Well,' the redhead said, 'if you're not throwing me in jail, where is the best place to stay?'

Rod Westerway's suggestive grin implied the bunkhouse at the Flying B but he didn't put his choice into words and the girl ignored him.

'I need to be where the biggest poker games are

being played,' she said.

Fred Onslow explained that there wasn't enough money in Beecher Gulch for games to be played for big pots but, as for hotels, she had a choice of two. The Bright Star, he concluded, was the best and most expensive. What he didn't tell her was that, due to a fire, it might be difficult to find a room there. Some of the displaced settlers waiting for the next train east had chosen to rent rooms rather than sleep outdoors in a tent. But he was sure she would find a room some-where. She looked respectable even if she had been thrown off the train.

The train gave a whistle: an indication that it was about to restart its journey, and those still standing on the platform stepped clear as it pulled away. The sta-tionmaster, who had been aboard the caboose while it was in the station, returned to his office with the deliv-ery of mail sacks.

Rod Westerway, who had come to the station to send a telegraph message to Cheyenne on behalf of Carl Benton, decided it was time to get back to the ranch. The boss of the Flying B would be interested to know that more settlers had arrived in the town.

The redhead walked down the street with Dan and the sheriff. The Bright Star was the first hotel they reached. To the manager's knowledge it had never before been so full, however there were still rooms available. The redhead signed the register as Linda Fellowes and received the key for room 19. Dan, who had entered the hotel with her, collected his own key.

They were along the same corridor, two doors apart.

'Do you play poker, Deputy?' asked the girl as he was about to open his door.

'It has been known,' he told her.

'Then perhaps we'll meet again at the tables.'

'But you are a hustler, a professional gambler. What chance would I have?'

'You shouldn't judge my character on one bad report,' she told him.

'That's true,' he agreed, 'but I expect to be busy for the next day or two.'

# CHAPTER SEVEN

It had been a long day for the people of Beecher Gulch, who had fought a fire, helped to resite the displaced families and had still found time to attend to the essential elements of their own occupations. When dusk fell, however, the men were able to shake off their weariness and congregate in the saloon. Indeed, the room was more full than usual; townspeople mingled with the original camp-dwellers, who were joined by those curious recent arrivals who were eager to understand the processes and practices that would quicken their acceptance in the territory. The hubbub raised by the countless conversations could be heard at the far end of town.

For a second night Dan Freemont entered the saloon in search of a poker game, and for a second night he became embroiled in a conversation with Sam Shaughnessey and Tom Keogh. The power of Sam's voice and the gravity of its tenor soon began to quell the talk of those around him. He was expounding on a revelation by a young lad which, if true, meant that the fire had been started deliberately. While Dan had been out at the Riddle place, the lad had disclosed that he'd seen men among the tents with firebrands. They had ridden away as soon as the alarm had been raised.

Shaughnessey didn't doubt the story for a moment. Stridently, he denounced Carl Benton, insisting that burning out the settlers was the next step in the cowman's efforts to chase away small landowners.

'Another two dead.' He emphasized his words by smashing his right fist into the palm of his left hand. 'First Ben Riddle murdered and now Mrs Galway and her child.' He spoke again, his voice rising above the murmurs of agreement. 'This can't go on. It can't go unanswered.'

Some men refused to believe that Benton would be so ruthless, arguing that they had done nothing to arouse such action, but in general, most people were swayed by the big Irishman's views. Few, however, welcomed the prospect of escalating violence, declaring they were farmers, not fighters. A suggestion that they should urge Sheriff Onslow to act on their behalf was ridiculed by Shaughnessey.

'What has he done about the killing of Ben Riddle? Nothing. He tells us he needs proof but I don't see him doing anything to get it.'

'We have to give him time,' someone called out. 'I don't suppose the man wants this sort of trouble any more than we do.'

'Perhaps we should all ride out to Benton's ranch,' someone else suggested. 'If we go as a united group then perhaps he'll realize that he isn't going to get his own way.'

'I'd advise against that unless you are prepared to fight fire with fire,' Dan Freemont said. 'Any show of force will give him the excuse to retaliate. Then you'll have a war on your hands.'

'That's what we already have,' said Shaughnessey, his tone making it clear that he disapproved of Dan's interference. 'If he's prepared to burn us out when we are all together then how ruthless will he be when we move on to our own individual strips?'

Dan's reply, that the sheriff was a good man who would do the right thing if he was allowed to handle the matter in his own way, had little influence on the gathering. Indeed, because Shaughnessey's prediction resonated in his own mind, he was barely able to put any conviction into his words. In normal circumstances he wouldn't have interfered in the dispute; he had no interest in a town that would soon be left behind in his dust, but something had made him speak up and he attributed it to friendship that had been shown to him by the sheriff and his family.

Shaughnessey glowered at those nearest, leery of the possibility that those reluctant to fight would be swayed by Dan's comments. Before he could come up with another argument, however, the batwings were pushed heavily aside and the appearance of three men brought to the room to silence.

For a moment Chas Tulley and two other riders on Benton's payroll stood in the doorway, then Tulley led the way towards the counter. A path was created for them, men stepping aside, pressing back against their friends and neighbours until the centre of the room was an empty space.

Shaughnessey, pushing away from the bar and flexing his shoulders and chest to advertise his size and strength, stared at the new arrivals as though preparing to challenge their right to be in the saloon. Tulley allowed his hand to slip to the butt of his revolver, a silent threat to the unarmed Irishman.

'I'm not armed,' said Shaughnessey, 'but nor am I frightened of you.' Even so, he stepped aside so that the Flying B men could reach the bar.

Tulley grinned, full of confidence because of his reputation as a fast gun. He lifted his head and sniffed, turned around so that he faced the men in the room while addressing his companions who had joined him at the counter.

'A strong smell of smoke in here tonight.'

Throughout the room, the taunt provoked grumbles of protest but few of the men were armed and none were prepared to confront Tulley.

'What kind of tobacco are you farmers rolling? It smells like old canvas.'

'Tulley,' said Dan Freemont, 'I suggest you finish your drink and hit the trail home.'

'Well, Deputy, is that an official order?'

'It's advice that you should take.'

'And if I don't want to go what do you intend to do about it?'

'Don't be a fool, Tulley. Don't start trouble in a room full of men who think you are responsible for the death of one of their friends.'

Tulley barked a short laugh. 'These men? They won't do anything. They haven't the courage. But what about you, Deputy? You haven't got the Irishman's excuse of not being armed. Do you think you can make me leave town?'

Again Tulley lowered his hand so that it hovered near his gun's ivory handle. Dan Freemont knew that he was unlikely to win a contest with a regular gunman, but while he'd been talking he'd manoeuvred himself to a position alongside the counter and less than two yards from Tulley.

'I can try,' he said, and instantly swept up Tulley's whiskey glass and tossed the contents into his eyes.

Caught by surprise and with the alcohol stinging his eyes, Tulley's reaction was slow. His right hand reached for his gun while his left arm was raised to his face in an effort to ease the irritation in his eyes. Partially blinded, he was incapable of avoiding the assault launched at him by Dan Freemont.

Immediately after throwing the drink, Dan threw a punch that connected heavily with Tulley's jaw. The cowboy staggered backwards, scattering the nearest men and colliding with a small card table. Unable to regain his balance, he fell to the floor. He shook his head to clear his senses of the effects of the initial blow and tried once more to pull his gun from its holster. Dan, meanwhile, had followed his adversary across the room, fully aware that he couldn't allow him to get the pistol clear of leather. He dived forward, his left hand reaching out to grab the other's gun hand while, at the same time, his right fist again struck Tulley's jaw.

Tulley grunted but maintained his senses. His gun was almost free of the holster, but Dan's hold on his right wrist was strong. Even if he withdrew the gun entirely it was unlikely that he would be able to get into an effective firing position. Unsuccessfully he struggled, tried to shift Dan's weight so that he could throw a punch of his own, twisting one way then the other, but he couldn't budge the bulk of Dan's body.

Then there was a moment of relief as Dan shifted position, first of all kneeling in what seemed to be a precursor to gaining his feet, then relaxing his hold; this fooled Tulley into thinking that he had an opportunity to draw his gun. In fact, it was a ploy to enable Dan to adjust his hold so that he was then able to disarm Tulley by bending back his wrist almost to breaking point.

The released gun clattered to the floor. Dan clambered to his feet and by dragging on the other's shirt, pulled Tulley up after him. He hit him with two right-hand blows, the first sinking deep into his opponent's stomach, causing him to fold, thereby lowering his head on to the second punch which landed on the side of his face.

Once again, as Tulley reeled across the room, bystanders scattered, clearing a way along which he stumbled before collapsing on to the floor. For a moment he remained in an ungainly heap. He gave another shake of his head, swiped a hand across his mouth to wipe away the blood that covered it, then cast a glare at his opponent, which carried the message that he wasn't yet beaten. His eyes searched the floor for his pistol and lighted on it just as Dan Freemont kicked it into a far corner.

Tulley reached down and from his boot produced a long-bladed knife. He threw himself forward, giving Dan no time to reach for his own gun at his side, and attacked furiously with a long, downward swipe. Dan moved nimbly, stepping backwards to avoid the slash that would have opened him from left shoulder to right hip if it had connected. But although he'd escaped that first sally he knew that his opponent now had the upper hand. Without a moment's hesitation Tulley launched another attack, swiping left to right and back again, the weapon's tip failing to rip open Dan's belly by little more than the thickness of his shirt.

With his back against the counter Dan reached out, caught Tulley's arm, but the hold he gained was insubstantial and easily shaken away. Dan kicked out, caught Tulley on the knee, which caused him to curse and stagger but he was still no more than two steps away and had adopted the semi-stoop that was characteristic of many knife fighters. It was a killing stance, and as he held Dan's gaze with his own he flipped the knife from hand to hand, a proven method of confusing an opponent, throwing doubt in his mind as to whether the next lunge would come from right or left.

Dan had already realized that he couldn't wait for Tulley to make the next move. He had to go for his own gun because shooting his opponent appeared to be his only means of escape. He knew he might not be fast enough, there was no guarantee that he could draw his gun more quickly than Tulley could lunge forward, but he knew for certain that if he did nothing he would be killed. His hand began its movement towards his hip but didn't complete the draw. A shot rang out and a familiar voice roared through the silence.

'Put down that knife, Tulley, or I'll put you down.' The bulk of Fred Onslow came into Dan's focus behind Chas Tulley's right shoulder. 'What's happening here?' he demanded.

Tulley didn't take his eyes from Dan's face. 'Nothing that won't keep for another day.'

'You're in enough trouble,' the sheriff told him. 'Get out of town. I'll throw you in jail if I see you around here before I send for you.'

After the trio from the Flying B had left the saloon, Shaughnessey slapped Dan on the back.

'It was a good fight until he pulled the knife. You should have shot him.'

'I would have done if I'd had the opportunity to pull my gun.'

'Then I'd be locking you in the jail,' Fred Onslow told him. 'I don't want any more killings in this town.'

'It's going to be hard to avoid,' said Dan. 'I'm told that last night's fire was started deliberately. If that's true, and it was on Benton's orders, there'll be more incidents until one side or the other hollers enough.'

Dan didn't play cards in the saloon. He had a drink with the sheriff but he couldn't get Sam Shaughnessey's words out of his mind. He had to agree that the attack on the settlers' camp, if instigated by Carl Benton, was a statement of intent that boded ill for any settler alone on land that the rancher considered his by right, and Sarah Riddle was one such target. Foreign as it was to his nature, he couldn't shake off the uneasiness he felt for her safety. Fred Onslow invited him to supper.

'Cora's been baking. She half-expected you to join us for dinner.'

Dan rejected the offer, his words delivered reflectively, emphasizing the fact that his mind was pre-occupied with other matters.

'I ate at the hotel.'

'Perhaps another time,' suggested the sheriff, who mistook the reason for Dan's lack of interest. 'Perhaps the person you expect to meet will arrive on Saturday's eastbound.'

'What? Oh, sure, sure.'

Fred Onslow made one more attempt to grab Dan's attention.

'I have something I want you to see. Call into the office tomorrow and we'll discuss it.'

Dan promised to do just that, then headed back to the Bright Star. His destination wasn't the hotel's bar or his bedroom, but the building at the rear, where his horse was stabled. He had decided to ride out to the

Riddle place. He had no explanation for the compulsion to do so, but knew that it wouldn't leave him if he remained in town. It wasn't his plan to disturb Sarah Riddle; he would observe her house without her knowledge and if his worries were groundless then she would never know the role he'd undertaken.

As he passed the front of the hotel he was hailed from the darkness of the long veranda.

'Good evening, Deputy.' It was a female voice, cultured and friendly and it caused Dan to break his stride. Linda Fellowes emerged from the shadows. 'It seems the sheriff was right about the shortage of money in this town,' she told him. 'I haven't seen as much as a deck of cards since I arrived. Perhaps I'll go down the street. There must be a game in progress in one of the saloons.'

Dan shook his head. 'Stay in the hotel,' he advised, 'you'll be safer there. No one is playing poker tonight. Trouble's brewing in this town.'

'What kind of trouble?' she asked.

The tone of her voice surprised Dan, conveying to him the thought that her inquisitiveness was more than the ploy of a bored woman seeking to prolong a conversation. She'd lifted her head to gaze along the street in the direction of the saloon, as though expecting to see some evidence of the trouble predicted by Dan. By the dim light of the hotel lamps he studied her, approved of her face and figure and detected in the set of her mouth and questing gaze a strength of character that he could admire.

He'd met other women who were professional gamblers and was aware that they were as stigmatised by mistrust as their male counterparts, and were no less susceptible to the threat of violence when winning money from those who believed they'd been cheated. It made those women watchful, prudent and careful to avoid situations that could lead them into trouble. The look on Linda Fellowes's face, however, showed no fear, just an interest in knowing more of the trouble that she'd been told was hanging over Beecher Gulch.

Dan had heard the names of many gamblers who worked the railways but Linda Fellowes was not among them. In other circumstances he would have been eager to play against her, test her abilities and her nerve, but on this night he had more important business.

'The kind of trouble that always comes when a man of influence is afraid of losing his power,' he answered. 'He adopts whatever tactics he feels necessary to hold on to what he has.'

With that, Dan tipped his hat and moved on towards the stable.

On the crest between the field of growing corn and the farm buildings there was a stand of three cottonwoods, among which Dan Freemont stood guard. There were two buildings, the larger one being Sarah Riddle's home and the smaller a shelter for the animals. In the absence of a ready supply of wood and stone, the buildings had been constructed by piling regular bricks of thick prairie sod, covering them with oiled paper, then plastering the finished walls with a lime-based stucco. They were adequate homes but susceptible to damp and in constant need of repair. Dan thought of all the heavy work that would be Sarah Riddle's lot if she remained on this strip of land.

He was about 300 yards from the buildings and, as the night began to grow colder, he wrapped a blanket around his shoulders. Wedged between two of the trees, he had a view of the house to his right and the route from the river to his left. Cradled in his arms was his rifle which had a full magazine of nine bullets. Drowsiness, encouraged by the darkness and silence of the night began to dissipate the presentiment that had drawn him out of Beecher Gulch.

He was beginning to feel foolish; he had rejected the company of a pretty young girl and an intriguing, beautiful woman to wait out on the cold prairie because of an inexplicable, probably groundless, foreboding. Sarah Riddle's safety, he told himself, wasn't his concern. Indeed, she might be as much alarmed by the fact that he was loitering within a quarter of a mile of her home as she would be by his unsubstantiated belief that her home might come under attack. He yawned, which annoyed him; some guard he would be if he couldn't stay awake!

He stretched and considered a patrol to keep him active. The house was silent, so he would walk to the crop field and back. But then his horse tossed its head and snickered. It had caught a scent on the breeze. He cast aside the blanket draped around his shoulders, put his hand over the horse's muzzle and waited for his own senses to assure him that other people were abroad.

The first confirmation was the sound of hoofbeats. More than one horse was approaching from the river at a cautious speed. Dan peered into the darkness and worked the rifle's mechanism as he did so, ensuring that it was ready to fire if the situation demanded such action. The pace of the horses began to slow and when they stopped Dan could discern three riders almost parallel to his own position.

For a while they were still, observing the buildings ahead, and if they spoke they did so in low murmurs because the night breeze carried no voices to him. Then they moved, changing formation from the line they had been in to a close huddle, the purpose of which at first eluded Dan.

Then a spark flew into the blackness of the night and Dan understood its meaning. One of the trio had a tinder box. In a moment a flame blossomed and within seconds all three riders brandished burning torches. With a yell they put their mounts to the gallop.

Instantly, Dan ran from the protection of the trees and shouted his own warning as he raised his rifle to his shoulder. A pistol barked in the still night but the bullet that had been fired at Dan was well away from its mark. Using the burning brand as a marker, Dan fired at the nearest raider. The man threw up his arms and fell heavily from his horse. Surprised by the apparent ambush, the other two riders drew rein to put an end to their attack on the soddy. Words were exchanged and another shot was fired at Dan. Again, he returned fire with success. One of the riders shouted with pain, dropped his flaming torch and swayed in the saddle as he headed at speed back towards the river. The third man, close behind his wounded comrade, realised that the flame he was carrying made him a target that couldn't be missed by such a capable gunman. His torch, too, was flung aside as he raced his partner to the river.

With the hammer of his rifle pulled back, Dan collected one of the torches and looked down at the raider who remained on the ground. With arms outspread, Chas Tunney looked at the black sky with unseeing eyes.

# CHAPTER EIGHT

During the remaining hours of darkness Sarah Riddle kept to her house. No lamp was lit, no challenge made to discover the cause of the disturbance in her yard, and no attempt was made by Dan Freemont to appraise her of the situation, although twice he had seen the ghost of her face at a window. Explanations would follow when she could be sure of his identity.

At sunup Dan employed himself by harnessing the team to Sarah Riddle's flat wagon and hoisting Chas Tulley's body on to its bed. When he was done he found the widow standing at the open door with a scatter gun in her hands, the barrels pointed at the ground. He told of her of the rumour in town that the burning of the camp had been a deliberate act to discourage settlers and that he'd considered it possible that they would try the same trick against her. Then he'd insisted that she returned to town with him.

'That dead man worked for Carl Benton,' he told her, 'which gives Sheriff Onslow a bit of leverage. It's possible that with that kind of evidence against him

Benton will stop his campaign against the settlers, but it's just as likely that he'll increase it. I think matters are coming to a head and it'll be safer for you in town for a few days.'

Sarah Riddle was reluctant to leave but Dan wasn't prepared to give an inch.

'It doesn't mean that you are forsaking your homestead; the land is still yours and Benton will be charged with trespass if he tries to run cattle on it, but the sheriff and I can't be here full time. You'll be safer among the townsfolk until the matter is settled.'

Their arrival in Beecher Gulch was watched with interest by several people. It was, at first, with professional interest that Zach Hartnell looked up from the anvil where he was shaping a horseshoe. There was a distinctly false note in the sound of an approaching iron-rimmed wheel and he was always alert for the prospect of another customer. The sight of Dan Freemont sitting alongside Ben Riddle's widow at such an early hour aroused base speculation. Although the newcomer had no long-term plans to stay in Beecher Gulch, it seemed that he wasn't losing any time in pressing his attention on Sarah Riddle. Again, the thought flashed into Zack's mind that Fred Onslow had been misled into thinking that Carl Benton was the author of Ben Riddle's killing; that perhaps the man who was so eager for the company of the dead man's wife had played some part in her widowhood.

Zach would have returned to hammering the hot metal but Theo Dawlish had begun waving to him.

Theo, it was clear, had seen something of interest in the back of the passing wagon and was casting aside the brush that was habitually in his hands when he had no customers to attend to, in order to follow the vehicle along the street. Other people, too, were walking alongside the wagon, gossiping with each other, throwing questioning glances at the couple on the driving board, but they were clearly receiving no word of enlightenment.

Outside the Bright Star Linda Fellowes observed the interest that had been aroused by the newly arrived wagon. It wasn't until it halted outside the sheriff's office that she recognized the driver and recalled their last conversation. He'd warned her of trouble in the town and, judging by the now animated reactions of some people who'd been drawn to the wagon, he'd brought some with him.

Cora Onslow had, that morning, delivered a basket containing pie and coffee to her father's office. It wasn't a regular practice and, grateful though he was for her offering, Fred Onslow suspected that his daughter's visit was more in the hope of finding Dan Freemont in his company. He was right, but when she joined her father on the boardwalk to find out the reason for the hubbub in the street, her happy mood was checked. Like Zach Hartnell, she was able to draw only one conclusion from the sight of Dan alongside Sarah Riddle at this early hour. While, the previous night, she'd prepared dinner, he'd found better entertainment at the home of the new widow and had stayed all night. She struggled to keep the pain she felt from showing on her face, but a call from the back of the wagon meant that her distress was neither noticed nor of interest to the gathering.

'It's Chas Tulley,' Zach Hartnell informed the sheriff. 'He's been shot.'

'Did you do it?' Fred asked Dan. There was a hint of anger in the lawman's expression, or disappointment, as though the killing had been an underhand act or had been done as a consequence of the previous night's fight.

'Yes.'

Hearing that answer, Fred Onslow ordered him into the office. Dan obeyed, accompanied by Sarah Riddle.

'Where did it happen?' Sheriff Onslow wanted to know.

'Out at Mrs Riddle's place.'

The sheriff looked from one to the other hoping they would volunteer the information he needed, but when neither Dan nor Sarah spoke he asked Dan why he had been out there.

'Sam Shaughnessey convinced me that if the tent camp had been burned deliberately then it was probable that those to blame would use similar tactics against settlers on their own land. I was concerned for Mrs Riddle. Her strip is the nearest to Carl Benton's land, which made her a likely victim. I camped out near her house. Three of them came to burn her out.'

'Three! Did you recognize the others?'

'It was too dark, but my guess would be those two with him in the saloon last night. I wounded one of them, no doubt you'll find him at Carl Benton's place.'

The sheriff gave Dan a twisted grimace, a look which said that he understood what Dan expected him to do.

'You want to ride out with me?' he asked. 'We need to take the body out there. Tulley is their responsibility.'

Dan said he would be happy to go with the sheriff after some accommodation had been found for Mrs Riddle.

'She's agreed to stay here until the threat to her safety is over.'

An hour later they met once more in the office. Cora was with her father when Dan arrived and her greeting had little of the warmth of their previous encounters.

'Because of the fire, the raising-bee at the Keoghs' place has been postponed,' she told him, 'so you're free to find whatever company you will tomorrow.'

Cora left abruptly, leaving a bemused Dan staring at the hastily closing door.

Cora's father smiled. 'When it's clear you've been at a widow woman's home all night you can't be surprised if people jump to conclusions.'

'I wasn't at Mrs Riddle's home,' Dan protested, 'I was camped on her land but she didn't know I was there until I'd put the harness on the horses to bring her into town.'

'Not my concern,' said Fred, 'as long as you're not making a fool of my daughter.'

Dan was on the point of protesting but the sheriff had pulled a newspaper from his drawer and laid it on his desk.

'This is what I wanted to show you,' he told Dan, but his words were unnecessary.

The headline announced the murder of Henry Garland in Scottsbluff, Nebraska, but a large portion of the remainder of the page was taken up with an image of the suspected killer. Dan was looking at his own face.

'No point denying that I'm the man they're looking for,' he told the sheriff, 'but I didn't do it.'

'Nothing I can do about it if you did. I haven't any authority to arrest anyone for crimes committed in Nebraska.'

'You could inform the authorities where I am,' Dan answered, 'but there's no need to do that. I'm supposed to be meeting a US marshal here, to tell him what happened.'

'The trains!'

'Yes, the trains. I'm not sure who is coming or where they are coming from. Perhaps he won't come at all.'

'You could have confided in me,' said Fred Onslow.

'I didn't think I'd be so long in your town.'

'And now you're involved in our troubles, or is it just the troubles of one woman?'

Dan refused to answer that question, joking instead about the sheriff wanting to engage a wanted man as his deputy.

'Still do,' Fred Onslow told him and, from another drawer, he took out a badge and handed it to Dan. 'Arresting somebody with one of those pinned to your chest emphasizes your authority. We'll need every advantage we can get when we face Carl Benton.'

They went out through the back door of the jail so that their departure didn't arouse the interest of those settlers who were hanging around town. The circumstances surrounding the death of Chas Tulley were being talked over and the volatile atmosphere that had been raised by Sam Shaughnessey the previous night was beginning to surface again. While Sheriff Onslow would have appreciated a posse of reliable officers riding with him he didn't want a rabble who might trigger off a deadly gun battle. He had Dan Freemont at his side and was confident that his presence would be sufficient.

Two miles from the Flying B they met Doc Pope heading in the opposite direction. He told them he'd been called to the ranch to pull a lump of lead out Jake Potter's shoulder. His patient had a broken collarbone but he would live. Jake Potter had been one of the two men who'd been with Chas Tulley in the saloon the previous night.

The other one was a fellow called Carter, who was among a small group gathered in front of the ranch house to identify the body draped over the Flying B-branded horse when it was led into the yard by Fred and Dan. Carter kicked the ground in a nervous fashion, his glance flicking regularly to the porch where Carl Benton observed the visitors to his ranch. Rod Westerway stood at the ranch-owner's side.

Fred Onslow spoke first as he cast aside the lead rein of the dead man's horse.

'Your man. He was killed in the execution of a crime and we mean to take the other two who were with him back to town.'

'They aren't in my employment.'

'Yes they are. That's why we're here.' The sheriff turned slightly in the saddle so that he was looking directly at Carter. He stretched out his left arm. 'That's one of them. Get your pony, fellow, because you're coming with us.'

Carter shuffled from one foot to the other, looked to Benton for assistance or guidance while his face showed fear at the prospect of being held in the small Beecher Gulch jail.

'You'll need to throw a saddle on Jake Potter's pony, too, because he's coming with us.'

'Jake's out at the north line cabin,' Jake Westerway announced.

Fred Onslow ignored him; he spoke to Carl Benton. 'These boys face serious charges. I'll make sure that anyone who gives false alibis to assist them is charged as an accomplice.'

'What are the charges?' asked Carl Benton.

'It'll be murder if, in addition to last night's attack, they were responsible for the burning of the tents outside Beecher Gulch. There are two innocent lives to answer for.'

'You can't pin that on them.'

'They were with Tulley at the Riddle place when the same tactic was employed. That gives me the right to hold them and question them.'

'Mr Benton!' Carter's words were a plea for help. It didn't escape the sheriff's notice that it wasn't a proclamation of innocence.

'Drop your gunbelt, Carter,' Fred Onslow ordered, 'then get those horses. Someone bring Jake Potter out here and get him mounted.'

For a moment, no one moved, Benton paid their wages so they obeyed only his orders. An expression of smugness began to show on Benton's face, a hint that he was going to back up his foreman's claim and deny that Potter was on the ranch. Fred Onslow probed one of his vest pockets and extracted a small item which he held between thumb and forefinger. He held it up so that Benton could see it.

'I know he's here. Doc Pope dug this out of Potter's shoulder less than an hour ago. If it matches the bullet we took out of Tulley it will prove him guilty of the cowardly attack on Mrs Riddle.'

Benton gave no immediate order and, apart from the now anxious Carter, the mood of those standing around was difficult to judge.

'Let me assure you,' Fred Onslow said, his voice calm and authoritative, 'that the purpose of my visit here is well understood by the councillors of Beecher Gulch. If my deputy and I fail to return then they'll put into motion the necessary steps to secure the safety of the town. They are determined that a range war will not be allowed to develop. Stick to your own land, Benton. The new arrivals are here to stay and you have to conform to the law. I'm taking Carter and Potter back to Beecher Gulch to stand trial, so get them on their horses now.'

There was only a brief pause before Carl Benton gave a sign for horses to be saddled and for Jake Potter to be brought from the bunkhouse. Disarmed and mounted, they led the way out of the ranch yard on to the open grassland with Dan riding guard a horse length behind. Before joining them Fred Onslow fired a parting shot.

'If I discover that they were acting on your orders, Benton, then I'll be back, and I'll make sure that whatever punishment is doled out to them is doled out to you, too.'

Rod Westerway followed his boss indoors.

'What did Onslow mean about the town councillors? What could they do if we took control in town and chased away the settlers?'

'Perhaps they have some plan to barricade the town, or bring in the sheriff from Cheyenne or one of the Nebraskan towns. But one man is one man and hardly enough to handle all the trouble we'd be capable of throwing up.'

'That deputy was wearing a badge. Sim Taylor suspected he was a fast gun marshal brought in to help the sheriff. Do you think he was the one who killed Tulley?'

'It's possible,' said Benton, 'but neither Jake nor Carter could identify him. It was too dark and the torches they'd lit were only an advantage to the shooter.

By their light he was able to pick them off before they were able to use them on the house.'

'So what now? You thought Tulley's gun would be enough to scare away the homesteaders, but he's gone. We can't leave those men in jail. Carter is sure to talk and tell the sheriff that it was your idea to burn out the camp. He's as scared as a hen in a coop with just a fox for company.'

'Until a judge arrives in town they can't hold a trial. We have time to do something to stop them talking.'

'Are you planning a jail break?'

'I haven't decided yet, but whatever happens it must appear as though the Flying B isn't involved. Did you contact Jim Ford?'

'I sent a telegraph message to Cheyenne yesterday.'

'Good. I want you to ride there immediately. You should reach Cheyenne before dawn. Bring Jim and his men back here without delay. They are to wait outside town for my orders. Fred Onslow might think he has the upper hand but he'll learn the truth when I unleash Jim Ford against him.'

It was the best part of a hundred miles to Cheyenne and within the hour, Rod Westerway had begun the journey which, for the most part, involved following the railroad line east. He didn't hurry, he wouldn't be able to locate Jim Ford until the next day when the townsfolk would be about their business, besides which he wasn't anxious to set himself afoot in the dark by incurring some needless accident on his horse.

\*

As had been their tactic when quitting Beecher Gulch earlier that day, Fred and Dan escorted their prisoners into the jailhouse via the back entrance. It was the sheriff's belief that the citizens would be less aggressive towards Jake Potter and Denny Carter if they'd been behind bars for more than a day before the fact of their arrest was made public.

When the iron-barred doors were closed and locked and the lawmen had settled down in the front office, Dan asked Fred the same question that Rod Westerway had asked Carl Benton.

'What plan do the town councillors have to prevent a range war?'

'Martial law,' was the reply. 'As you know, there are some limitations on the application of federal law in this territory which will remain until we're a state in the union, but Wyoming is still part of the United States of America, and in the event of civil unrest we can request the intervention of the army. The officer in command at Fort Collins is already aware of the situation, and if I'm unable to continue as sheriff then a message will be sent there and a cavalry unit dispatched immediately.'

Dan suggested that it was unusual for a town to seek martial law.

'The strict regulations and discipline that it brings are rarely welcomed,' he observed.

'What's the alternative? Allow the people of the town to choose sides and fight over the land? Now that the Indian wars are ended, the newcomers want to farm the land and build communities. They don't want to fight each other. But a fight is what they've got unless someone can arbitrate on their behalf with the cattlemen. In the absence of lawyers, that becomes the job of the peace officer, in the absence of a peace officer it's whoever can wield power impartially to preserve law and order.

'I've got a family. If I'm not able to protect them then I need to know that someone else will do it for me, and I'd prefer that they were annoyed by a few weeks of restrictions and curfews that lead to a settled future rather than a regime of war that might in the long-term benefit only a few.'

Dan couldn't argue with the sentiments of the sheriff, especially as it was still his expectation that he could soon be quitting the town. He volunteered for the night watch at the jail, promising to return after dinner. He had hoped to see Sarah Riddle in the dining room of the Bright Star but he learned later that she had taken a room in one of the hillside houses. Linda Fellowes was eating in the hotel, however, and she invited him to share a table.

'Perhaps tonight will be the night we play poker,' she said, but he answered that duty had to come before pleasure.

# CHAPTER NINE

It was by sheer chance that Jim Ford was crossing the street at the very moment that Rod Westerway pushed away his empty breakfast plate and looked out of the restaurant window. Barely an hour earlier Rod had arrived in Cheyenne, grubby and hungry, but now, with his horse stabled and his belly full, he was ready to set about the task of finding Jim Ford. Later in the day that would have involved a tour of the town's saloons, but early in the morning it was impossible to know where to look for him. Cheyenne was a large town and his was a name that was best not uttered without caution.

Jim Ford lived in this territory, where law enforcement was limited, because he operated with scant regard for the rights of others. He was a thief and a killer, wanted in three states, and he led a band of men of similar mien. Cheered by his luck, Rod Westerway pushed back his chair, selected some coins from his pocket to pay for his meal, then dashed into the street.

The cowman's approach didn't sit easily with Jim

Ford. He was more accustomed to clandestine meet-
ings in closed rooms where no one could overhear his
discussions. Being accosted openly in the street made
him wary, suspicious that he was being lured into some
lawman's trap. He glanced around to apprise himself
of anyone who might be taking special interest in their
meeting, but the few people abroad at that early hour
were intent on going about their own business.

'You're needed out at Beecher Gulch immediately,'
the foreman informed the outlaw. 'There's an initial
payment of two hundred dollars, and fifty dollars for
every man you bring along. There'll be a bonus for
every extra duty.'

'Only two of my men are in Cheyenne. A Colorado
posse killed or captured the rest last week. They nearly
got me, too,' Ford told him.

'Can't you find more?'

'Not if you want me to leave immediately. Difficult
to get men to join a gang who've been involved in such
a disaster.'

Rod Westerway pondered the situation, but it took
only a moment for him to conclude that he had no
option but to accept a reduced force. Carl Benton
would want Carter and Potter out of jail before a judge
arrived in Beecher Gulch, so it was too late to seek
assistance elsewhere.

'We need to be out of Cheyenne by midday,' he said.
'We'll meet at the livery stable.'

They were on the point of parting when their attention was drawn to a bunch of riders coming along the

street from the east. They were four in number and their dusty clothes and unshaved features made it clear that they had been travelling for several days. The horses, too, were moving wearily, their iron-shod hoofs barely lifting from the ground as they stepped forward to raise more dust and grit from the dirt street.

The lead man was tall and wiry. His dark shirt was stained with sweat marks and his trousers were flecked with lather from his horse's flanks. A grim scowl twisted his features as he slowed his animal to walking pace, a manoeuvre matched by his companions. As they reached the place where Jim Ford and Rod Westerway were in conversation the leader of the group cast a curious glance in their direction.

It didn't go unnoticed. Jim Ford, wary that the Colorado posse had crossed the border in pursuit, regarded the new arrivals with suspicion and his hand moved automatically towards the gun at his side. The horseman noted this movement and his hand too slipped to his holstered weapon. For a moment it seemed that the parties were on the verge of fiery violence, as though an exchanged glance had given birth to a bitter enmity. Then the rider relaxed and a grin spread over his face.

'Is that you, Jim?'

'Gatt Peters! I thought you were still in Mexico.'

Since the end of the war, when both men had ridden with Archie Baker, each had changed his name. Gatt Peters had become Gatt Hardin and Jim Taylor had become Jim Ford. Remembrance of those days briefly rekindled their former companionship but the years of hiding and subterfuge had affected their characters to such an extent that neither chose to talk freely about the intervening years. Meeting at the present time, however, was mutually acceptable.

'What are you doing in Cheyenne?' Jim Ford wanted to know.

'We are looking for someone on behalf of a friend of yours.'

It took a moment for Jim Ford to realize the significance of Gatt's words. Because he hadn't heard of Archie Baker for several years he had assumed that, if the guerrilla leader was still alive, he had quit the United States altogether.

'You hope to find him in Cheyenne?'

'Not really. We don't know where to look. We thought he was in Nebraska or Colorado but we haven't been able to pick up his trail.'

'Why not join me?' said Jim Ford. 'I need some good men to come to Beecher Gulch for a few days. Fifty dollars for each of you immediately, with the prospect of more.'

Gatt shook his head. 'We're only here so that I can send a telegram. Perhaps we'll have a day of rest, but then we'll have to carry on with our search.'

One of the other riders, a younger man with a twisted lip, spoke up, commenting that fifty dollars sounded good to him. 'We've been chasing around for days and not getting any closer to catching the gambler. We would all benefit from a bit of action.'

'Be quiet, Dutton. You're already being paid to do a job.'

'I'm leaving in the next hour or two,' Jim Ford said. 'If you change your mind you'll find me at the livery stable.'

'If you need more time to consider the matter,' chimed in Rod Westerway, 'there's a train to Beecher Gulch tomorrow. I'll reimburse you for the price of the ticket if you decide to join us.'

Gatt Hardin said he wouldn't change his mind. He rode on down the street to the telegraph office with the other three in his wake.


After leaving Ogallala, the foursome had ridden to Julesburg then on to Greeley without finding any sign to indicate they were on Dan Freemont's track. At Greeley Gatt had contacted Jason Whalley, whose instructions had brought them north into Wyoming. Scottsbluff was north-east of Cheyenne and another day and a half's ride would get them back to where they'd started.

It was probable though that Jason Whalley wouldn't want them to return. He'd been insistent that Freemont had to be caught and killed before they returned and. unless the other group that was scouring the territory east of Scottsbluff had had success in finding the fugitive, they would have to stay in the saddle for several more days.

Like Seb Dutton, Gatt was weary of the chase, but if the gambler revealed Jason Whalley's true identity then he too would be unmasked as a war criminal. That risk had lurked at the back of his mind ever since Archie Baker had taken on a politician's mantle but recently the matter had become nebulous, overshadowed by the thrust for power, until the events at Scottsbluff. He sent off his message knowing he was unlikely to receive a reply until the next day.

Seb Dutton wouldn't let the matter lie. 'We're not even chasing shadows, riding from town to town the way we are. Why don't we tell Jason Whalley that somcone claims to have seen the gambler in Beecher Gulch? That gives us a reason for going there. We can earn some money before numbing our butts with another pointless ten days in the saddle.'

'We need to wait for an answer to my telegraph message. It'll give instructions where to go next.'

'I'm not waiting,' insisted Seb. 'I want to catch that gambler as much as anyone else.' For emphasis, he rubbed the back of his head where it had been split open during the fight in the Scottsbluff stable. 'What we're doing is a waste of time. Send a message to Beecher Gulch when you move on and I'll rejoin you when I can.' He looked at the faces of the other three. 'Anyone with me?'

When it became clear that he was acting alone he left them and went in search of Jim Ford. Shortly after that five men rode westward out of Cheyenne towards Beecher Gulch.

Sheriff Onslow and the badge-wearing Dan Freemont

managed to keep the fact that they had men from the Flying B locked up in jail a secret for most of the day. Theo Dawlish and Zack Hartnell were informed of the situation, as was Doc Pope, who was needed to attend to the dressing on Jake's shoulder. The only other person to enter the sheriff's office that day was his daughter with a basket of food. Fred Onslow was grateful, it meant that there was no need to send out for food, which would have advertised the fact that he had prisoners in his cells. Cora was less pleased, once again the real object of her visit was absent. Dan was catching up on his sleep in his bedroom in the Bright Star.

When the eastbound train chugged past the Beecher Gulch platform without stopping, Dan was leaning against the ticket-office wall. Another day without contact. Once more he considered sending a message to Mark Clement in Ogallala. Then, as he moved towards the door, he found he was not alone. Standing there was Linda Fellowes.

'If you want to get aboard you have to tell the station master so that he can flag it down. It doesn't stop unless someone wants to get off,' he told her.

'I wasn't thinking of leaving,' said Linda Fellowes. 'Just heard the whistle, so I came to see if there were any new arrivals.'

'Are you expecting someone?'

She shook her head but it seemed to Dan that it was more of an evasion than an answer.

'I thought you would have been on your way by now,'

he said. 'There's nothing much to keep a big-time gambler here.'

She smiled at him. 'Too true. I haven't won enough to buy a ticket to the next town.'

He looked her over and admired the maroon check outfit she was wearing.

'You don't look as though you're starving.'

'Was that a compliment, Deputy?'

'I'm not sure it was anything but a statement of fact. However, if you choose to take it as a compliment I have no objection.'

'How gallant,' she said. 'Perhaps I'll allow you to share my dinner table again.'

'Not tonight. Duty calls again. I have to be in the office tonight.'

'Perhaps I'll call in,' she said. 'While away an hour or two with a pack of cards.'

Such a proposition required little consideration.

'I'll expect you about nine.'

Sarah Riddle had filled Dan's thoughts since he'd chased Fred Onslow home and taken up his station behind the lawman's big desk. He hadn't seen the widow since bringing her to Beecher Gulch and, more important, he hadn't fulfilled the promise he'd made to fix the fence that had been torn down. Events had conspired to keep him otherwise occupied and until the trial was over the situation wouldn't change. By then the arrival of a US marshal would surely have had a significant influence on his immediate future. His thoughts were interrupted by Linda Fellowes's light tap on the office door.

For almost an hour they played, Dan reaching the conclusion that although she was a capable player Linda Fellowes wouldn't win much money in the high-stakes games that he was accustomed to. Perhaps, he decided, hustling on railcars, where her looks would be enough to pull the wool over most men's eyes, was the extent of her ability. But she was good company and they were laughing loudly when they were disturbed by another knock on the door.

Cora Onslow, bringing her second basketful of food that day, flushed with anger when she set eyes upon the elegant redhead who was proving such an affable companion for the man she knew as Dan Bayles.

'Well, no wonder you didn't want to join me for dinner,' Linda Fellowes declared, 'when such fare is brought to your door.' Whether Linda's remarks were intended to inflame Cora only she would know, but the younger woman could barely contain her anger.

'Perhaps I should tell my father that being a deputy is interfering with your social life. After tonight I suggest you let *him* stay here overnight.'

'No need for that, Cora. We're only playing cards.'

Cora cast a glare at Linda Fellowes, who was examining the contents of the basket.

'Doesn't matter to me what you do,' she declared, 'and that food is for the prisoners.'

Linda looked at Dan, then at Cora and gave a slight shrug.

'I've already had supper,' she said. 'Perhaps it's time I returned to the hotel.' She wrapped a shawl around her shoulders, went outside and closed the door.

'Is that really for the prisoners?' Dan asked, 'because it smells better than anything I've had since I had dinner with your family.'

Cora didn't have the opportunity to answer because once more there was a knock at the door. Dan stepped across the room to answer it.

Unlike his journey to Cheyenne, Rod Westerway's return to Beecher Gulch was made in the best possible time. With a rhythmic pace, the mounts of the five riders devoured the miles and they reached the outskirts of Beecher Gulch before dusk. Rod Westerway left Jim Ford and his companions to make camp about three miles outside town, then crossed the river to report to his boss at the Flying B ranch. Carl Benton was happy to see his foreman: he had a plan he wanted to put into action that night.

'A judge is expected on tomorrow's westbound train and I can't risk Potter and Carter appearing before him.'

'You want them to escape tonight?'

'No. I want something more final than that. Patch Reid was in town earlier. According to him the settlers don't know that the sheriff has Potter and Carter in his jail. Get Ford to spread the word around town tonight and with whiskey inside the settlers it ought to be easy enough to incite them to a lynching.'

'Carter and Potter?'

'They've served their usefulness.'

Benton's blunt abandonment of his men shocked the foreman. The boss of the Flying B had always been a tough employer, had ensured that he got full worth for the dollar a day he usually paid, but he had always been fair with those who were loyal to him. Now, beset by troubles brought about by the influx of settlers, his behaviour was becoming more dictatorial and this latest example of his ruthlessness marked an attitude that he intended to win at any cost.

'Why would anyone take heed of Ford? He'll be a stranger in town.'

'That's why the idea will work. The town is full of strangers. Those who came in on the last train will think he's from the tent camp and the tent-dwellers will think he came in on the train. All he has to do is to tell them that the men in the jail started the fire that killed the woman and her child. That accusation is sure to give rise to others, that is the nature of a mob. Sheriff Onslow's treatment of the settlers will be less sympathetic if they lynch his prisoners. And perhaps,' he added, 'the good sheriff won't escape unscathed.'

So Rod Westerway rode out to Ford's camp, gave the men a summary of the events that had led to the imprisonment of Carter and Potter, then supplied each man with a handful of dollars with which to buy the necessary alcohol.

'Remember you are meant to be settlers,' he told them, 'so go armed only with rope for the hangings.'

*

Later that night, in the saloon, the plan was set in motion. The four men mixed with the other customers, listened to their conversation and complaints and identified the most volatile, those most likely to react in a manner that would result in a riot. Glasses were filled and refilled, a word of incitement uttered here and there, then came the disclosure that those responsible for the fire that had taken two lives and put the whole town in peril were being held in the sheriff's cells.

It was barely necessary to add the further fuel that those same men had attacked a lone woman, forced her off her land and would visit the same treatment on every man and his family if they were not stopped now.

One or two voices attempted to calm the situation, but were soon drowned by the clamour for revenge. Torches were lit, coils of rope appeared and the mob moved out of the saloon en route for the jail.

When Dan opened the door he was surprised to find Linda Fellowes standing there, but, even as she alerted him to the approaching mayhem, the burning brands borne in its midst had grabbed his attention, and the shouts and murmurings that arose from the mob carried to him on the still night air.

'Get to the hotel,' he told her, and pushed her so that he could reclose the door.

'No,' she said, and, catching him by surprise, she pressed past him into the jailhouse.

'What are you doing?' he demanded. 'That's a lynch mob. Get out of here.'

But Linda Fellowes was ignoring him, making herself useful by closing the wooden shutters over the windows.

'Quickly,' he said. 'Out the back.' He turned to Cora. 'Get your father. It seems that someone has discovered that we're holding prisoners in the cells.'

Cora looked from Dan to Linda Fellowes. Though her face betrayed signs of fear there was also an expression of doggedness: if the redhead was staying then she was too. Dan unlocked the rear door.

'Quickly, Cora. I need your father here now.' The young girl nodded and darted out into the night.

'You, too,' Dan told Linda. 'I don't want to worry about you.'

'You don't have to,' she told him.

The tumult from the approaching group was increasing and Dan had no time left to argue with her. He grabbed a shotgun from the wall rack, checked that both barrels were loaded, then crossed the room to the door. He turned back to look at the redhead. It was clear that she was aware of the danger heading her way, but she remained calm and nodded her head as a sign that she trusted his judgement and that she wouldn't fail him.

'Lock this door behind me,' he told her. 'If things go wrong then get out by the back door as quickly as possible.' With those words he stepped outside.

Sam Shaughnessey was at the front of the crowd.

'We've come for the prisoners, Deputy. They killed Mrs Galway and her youngster. Hanging them is justice.'

'I'm not going to argue the finer points of law with you, Sam, I'm just telling you to go home. There'll be a judge here tomorrow and he'll decide on the rights and wrongs of the matter.'

A voice from the crowd yelled out: 'We all know the rights and wrongs,' and that sentiment received a chorus of support. Someone at the back of the mob urged everyone forward.

'What are we waiting for?' he shouted. 'We came here for the prisoners and one man isn't going to stop us.'

Again a great shout of approval greeted the speaker's words. Sam Shaughnessey stepped up on to the boardwalk in front of the sheriff's office.

'Get back, Sam. No one is going in there.'

'Deputy,' said Sam Shaughnessey, 'you put up a good fight against one man the other night, but you can't hope to beat all of us.'

'I'll beat as many as it takes,' Dan replied, 'and any man who tries to pass me will end up in a cell.'

Sam Shaughnessey laughed, turned to face the crowd to let them see the derision he held for Dan's last statement then swung his arm back. His hand had been formed into a great fist which was meant to hammer Dan to the ground.

Dan, however, had expected the manoeuvre. The punch was only beginning its arc when Dan's own offensive exploded on the big Irishman's skull. Gripping the shotgun by barrel and stock, Dan crashed it against Sam Shaughnessey and the man fell at his feet with a groan. Instantly, Dan fired one of the barrels into the air.

'Go home,' he yelled. 'If I have to empty the other barrel then some of you will get hurt.'

Dan had hoped that the brief flurry of violence would be sufficient to defuse the situation, but another man stepped forward, his face reddened by a combination of alcohol and passion. He made an effort to grab Dan's shotgun but all he got was its butt when it was jabbed ferociously into the pit of his stomach. He groaned as Dan pushed him back into the crowd but his action had given encouragement to others.

A lot of people were shouting and it was apparent to Dan that the mood of the crowd was building up to an attack which he knew he wouldn't be able to repel. He was reluctant to discharge the second barrel into the crowd, but it was becoming increasingly likely that that would be his only hope of survival.

A second shotgun blast roared in the darkness, once more a shot flew high over everyone's heads, stilling the mob. Dan had not been responsible for that discharge, it had come from the jail, where the barrels of another weapon had been thrust through a slot in the window shutter.

In the silence that followed, Fred Onslow emerged from the side of the building and stood shoulder to shoulder with the man who was acting as his deputy. He, too, held a shotgun, which was pointed at the crowd.

Someone at the back tried to maintain the impetus

that had brought the mob to the door of the jail but Sheriff Onslow advised against it.

'Not one more step,' he told them, 'or we'll make sure that you all get a taste of lead. You won't do much farming if you lose an arm or a leg or the sight of your eyes. Now get to your homes. The saloons are closed for the rest of the night.'

Amid low grumbles and comments the mob dispersed. Fred and Dan remained on the street until it was empty, then between them they hauled Sam Shaughnessey to the jailhouse door for a night in the cells. Fred Onslow's eyes opened wide with surprise when the door was opened by Linda Fellowes, but explanations, he decided, could wait until later.

# CHAPTER TEN

'You've got a hard head,' Sheriff Onslow told Sam Shaughnessey while pouring coffee from the pot that his daughter had brought earlier to the jail. 'With the clout my deputy gave you I didn't expect you to wake up until next week.'

Sam sat on the cot at the side of the cell, fingering the ugly swelling on his temple.

'That's a good man to have on your side in a fight,' he muttered. 'He deserves more respect than I gave him.'

'Were you the ringleader of that rabble, Sam?'

'Perhaps I was. I know I was good and angry that you had those boys in here.' His gaze drifted to the far cell where Denny Carter and Jake Potter were listening to the conversation.

'Who told you they were here?'

Sam rubbed at his head again. 'I don't know the man. Must have been among the bunch who came to town after the fire.'

'Do you know his name?'

Sam didn't; the only other information he could supply was that the man had arrived in town with plenty of money because he didn't allow anyone to stand at the bar with an empty glass.

'You're here until the morning, Sam, then there'll be a fine to pay. If you take my advice you'll pay it without quibbling because if you're still in jail when the judge gets here he might not be so lenient. If he thinks you are guilty of violent disorder you could be transported to Fort Collins and imprisoned there for three years.'

Fred left the Irishman to ponder on the situation and confessed to Dan that he wasn't happy with the situation.

'In the morning I'll try to find this newcomer with money to burn, find out who told him that we were holding Potter and Carter in the cells.'

'Who knew?'

'You and me, my wife and daughter and Doc Pope.'

'Perhaps someone saw the doctor's visits and put two and two together.'

'Possible but unlikely. The doctor and I are old friends. He often pops in to pass the time of day.'

'Do you think there'll be another attempt to lynch them?' asked Dan.

'I doubt it. The situation will be defused if the judge gets here tomorrow. A trial will appease everyone.' He drank coffee from his mug, then looked around the room and realized that Linda Fellowes had returned to the hotel. 'What was the gambling lady doing here?' he asked.

'Gambling.' Dan's facetious answer didn't amuse the sheriff. 'You know who I am, a professional gambler who has had little opportunity to play a hand since reaching Beecher Gulch. It's hardly surprising that I'd grab the chance to play against another professional, even for penny stakes.'

'Perhaps she's the one who spread word about our prisoners.'

'I doubt it. I don't think the affairs of the town concern her.'

'Yet she stayed in the jail while you faced down a mob.'

'That wasn't my idea. I wanted her to leave with Cora.'

'I wonder why she didn't?' Fred Onslow decided that was a question he'd put to the lady herself when they next met.

Both sheriff and deputy remained in the office for the remainder of the night. Fred Onslow slept on a cot in one of his own cells while Dan Freemont dozed intermittently in the chair behind the big desk.

Carl Benton was furious when he learned of the failure of his scheme. Carter and Potter were still alive and their testimony was capable of putting a noose around his neck. He paced his room struggling mentally with his predicament. It was rumoured that the judge would be arriving on the next train, which meant that time was running out for the implementation of another plan. So, he concluded, if he couldn't eliminate them

134

then he had to buy their silence. He would visit them in jail, promise them riches if they kept his name out of the proceedings. It was still early in the morning but he poured a large whiskey because he needed the kick to steady his nerves.

Although the events of the previous night had left Carl Benton in a perilous position, for one of the riders he had brought in from Cheyenne they had turned out to be the key to a long fruitless search. From his position at the back of the mob Seb Dutton had, at first, doubted the evidence of his own eyes. The similarity between the man who had emerged from the sheriff's office to defy their demands and the gambler whom he had been hunting on behalf of Jason Whalley was remarkable. Yet it seemed impossible that in such a short period of time a man accused of a political assassination in a neighbouring state could be serving as deputy in a small frontier town.

Dutton had worked his way closer to the boardwalk, not close enough to arouse the interest of the deputy, but near enough to be sure of his identity. Once before they had been close enough to exchange blows, now any doubt that this was the man he had been seeking was dispelled. Had he been armed, had he ignored the foreman's instruction that settlers seldom carried guns, he could have put a bullet through the man's head. That would have resolved Whalley's problem, would have put the jail at the mercy of the mob and would have quenched his own need for revenge following the beating he had taken in the Scottsbluff stable.

However, at that moment he had not had the means to kill Dan Freemont and had been forced to quit the scene when the sheriff appeared with his loaded shotgun, but when the excitement had died down he had not quit the town along with his new companions. He'd hung around for two reasons. He wanted to confirm in the daylight that the deputy was Dan Freemont, then, at the earliest opportunity, he would send a telegram to Gatt Hardin in Cheyenne. *Catch the train,* it would read, *he's here.*

When the sun was up, when the traders had swept their boardwalk and opened their premises for business, Sheriff Onslow toured the street with a rifle tucked under his arm. He didn't expect to use it but he wasn't going to miss the opportunity to stress his authority in the town. The townsfolk, men like Theo Dawlish and Zach Hartnell, greeted him warmly, but the handful of settlers who had crossed the rails from the tent camp were reluctant to meet his accusing gaze. Their anger and bravado of the night before had become an embarrassment, accentuated by the dull headache that was the aftermath of too much rotgut whiskey.

Sam Shaughnessey accompanied Fred Onslow on his patrol. Always reluctant to spend the town's kitty on meals for undeserving prisoners, the sheriff had released the big Irishman without breakfast on the promise that he would pay the twenty-dollar fine before sundown and that he would point out the men whose words and money had incited the talk of lynching the previous night. When their search of the street proved fruitless they extended their hunt to the new tent camp. The men they were seeking weren't there either, and although most of those who had sore heads that morning recalled the men involved, no names were known. What was evident was that the men did not belong to the settlers who had been displaced by the fire, nor had they been amongst those who had recently arrived in Beecher Gulch.

'Which means,' Fred Onslow later told Dan, 'that they were sent into town with the sole intent of having the prisoners lynched.'

It was clear that only one man knew the identity of the prisoners and had something to gain from preventing them talking in a court of law. Sheriff Onslow had warned Carl Benton that the punishment would be severe if it could be proved that he was implicated in the attacks on the settlers, and Carter and Potter were probably capable of providing that evidence. Convinced that the owner of the Flying B had instigated the attempt to storm the jail, the sheriff presented his theory to his prisoners.

Frayed nerves had produced a long and sleepless night for Denny Carter and Jake Potter. The clamour of the crowd that had been intent on hanging them from the nearest high bar still echoed in their thoughts, and until the appearance of the sheriff and his deputy at their cell door their one crumb of comfort had been the belief that their boss wouldn't leave them in the Beecher Gulch jail when news of the outrage reached him.

They were shocked by the disclosure that the mob had been incited at his behest, and although, initially, they'd rejected the sheriff's interpretation of events, they were soon convinced of its truth. Carl Benton feared their testimony but now, with the lawman's promise to ask the judge for leniency, they admitted their guilt.

'We were acting on Mr Benton's orders,' Jake Potter admitted. 'He paid us fifty dollars to burn the settlers out of the territory.'

It was the confession that Fred Onslow needed to arrest Carl Benton. Dan Freemont insisted on riding out to the Flying B with him, so Zach Hartnell was drafted in to keep an eye on the jail while they were out of town.

Sim Taylor, herding cows on the river range, identified the sheriff and his deputy when they were still three miles from the ranch house. Their pace was unhurried yet purposeful, and he anticipated they'd come to take him into town to answer the charge of murder. He put his pony to a gallop and raced ahead to find Rod Westerway. The foreman was in the yard waiting for his boss to emerge from the house. Carl Benton had ordered him to saddle their horses because he was going into Beecher Gulch to talk to Carter and Potter in the town jail.

'They're coming for me.' As his pony slithered to a dust-raising halt, Sim Taylor couldn't disguise his anxiety. With the death of Chas Tulley he had become the principal suspect for the murder of Ben Riddle. His instinct for the past couple of days had been to flee westward, but Carl Benton had assured him that the sheriff's threat to stand him before a judge was nothing more than bluff.

'They have no proof that you were involved in the death of that land stealer,' the boss of the Flying B had declared, 'so they can't convict you. Your place is here. To run would suggest guilt.'

Sim had heeded his boss, had ridden out with the crew each morning and tried to pretend that he had nothing to fear but, despite Carl Benton's disdain for the law's ability to convict, he was haunted by the threat of the gallows. That morning, talk had centred around the homesteaders' attempt to drag Denny Carter and Jake Potter out of jail. Last night they had failed but the next time they might succeed and he might be the lynch mob's target.

'What should I do?' he asked the foreman.

Rod Westerway wasn't so sure that the lawmen were on their way to arrest Sim. It was possible that their visit was in connection with the previous night's events in Beecher Gulch. Only three of the gang had returned to Jim Ford's campsite after the failure to lynch Carter and Potter, so it was possible that the fourth man had somehow fallen foul of the law and revealed details of the plot. At that moment, Carl Benton stepped on to the veranda and prepared to climb aboard his horse.

'We've got visitors,' Rod told him and directed his

gaze towards the high gateway through which the lawmen were now riding.

Benton remained on the veranda, his head high, his chin jutted forward in obstinacy. He watched the approaching riders and remained silent when they reined their mounts to a halt at the steps that led up to the house. His employees remained mounted several yards to their left, Sim Taylor partly hidden by the foreman.

'I want your gun, Benton,' announced Fred Onslow, 'and yours, Sim Taylor. You're both under arrest and coming back to Beecher Gulch with me.'

Sim Taylor's eyes darted nervously, their gaze directed first at the lawman, then at his boss, then back to the lawman, whose own eyes were firmly fixed on the owner of the Flying B. Contemptuously, Carl Benton stared back.

'On what charge are you arresting me?'

'Murder. I told you I'd be back if you issued the orders that caused the death of Mrs Galway and her child.'

'I issued no such orders and you can't prove that I did.'

'On the contrary, Benton, I've got two signed affi-davits waiting to be presented to the judge when he arrives in town later today. He'll want an explanation if you are not waiting for him in one of my cells. Take a last look around the place; who knows if you'll see it again.'

Belligerently,     motionlessly,     the     cattleman

maintained his watch on the lawman.

'OK,' said Fred Onslow. 'Unfasten that belt around your waist and leave your gun there on the porch. Then get on your horse.'

'And if I don't?'

'I'll shoot you where you stand.'

The delay between the sheriff's words and the onset of action was only momentary. During that second Carl Benton considered and dismissed options, every instinct to fight his way out of the situation floundering on the dubious loyalty of his crew. If he drew a weapon, how would the drovers in the yard react? Could he even depend on his foreman shooting at the sheriff and his deputy, or would he be facing two guns alone. Fred Onslow wasn't a fast draw but nor was he, but the deputy had a reputation, and without assistance he had no hope of outshooting him. His eyes took in the fact that his foreman's hands were well away from his side arm, folded on the pommel of his saddle. His nerve failed him, he would unfasten his belt.

Rod Westerway sat motionless, unable to foretell Carl Benton's course of action and unsure of his own response if his boss resisted the lawmen. He had not been involved in the killing of Ben Riddle or in the arson attacks. The boss of the Flying B had given those orders directly to Chas Tulley. He was also aware that the man on his immediate right had already proved himself a marksman: he had no wish to die for another man's greed. He gripped the pommel more tightly.

Fred Onslow was tense as he watched the unbidden

tics and twitches that flitted across Carl Benton's face. He hadn't drawn his gun and he knew that to do so now would probably result in a gun battle that could take several lives, but his hand rested on his thigh, ready to draw his iron at the first suggestion that the boss of the Flying B meant to do likewise.

It was Sim Taylor, however, whose nerve broke first. The prospect of a hangman's loop frightened him, and if he was taken to Beecher Gulch there was little doubt but that that was the death that awaited him. Even if his neck wasn't stretched by a lynch mob he would be dropped through a gallows trapdoor at Fort Collins. He drew and fired in one clumsy movement, his shot missing Dan, the intended target, and striking Fred Onslow high in the chest. Close to unconsciousness, the sheriff slumped forward on to his horse's neck.

Carl Benton swore. With the passing years he had grown accustomed to being the decision maker, a position which ensured that everything that happened was for his benefit. The firing of Sim Taylor's gun meant that he was not the one in control. The gunshot could neither be recalled nor ignored; it was a call to battle to which both sides would respond. In less time than a heartbeat he found himself grabbing for the gun that he'd intended to discard.

While Fred Onslow had been confronting Carl Benton, Dan Freemont kept a wary eye on the two men mounted to his left, but, in common with the sheriff, at the moment of the gunshot the major part of his attention had been focused on the boss of the Flying B. He thought he'd glimpsed a weakening of the rancher's resolve, a blink that hinted at surrender, a hesitation in order to present an argument that would save face in front of his men, and his attention had been distracted from the activity of Sim Taylor and the foreman. It was probably due to the fact that, for the most part, Sim Taylor was obscured by Rod Westerway that he was able to draw his gun unobserved, but when it was fired Dan reacted with hitherto unknown alacrity.

He could never fully explain his actions nor was he able to understand how his subconscious was aware of so much information. It was almost as if he'd seen the bullet leave Sim Taylor's gun, had followed its progress as it clipped an ear of Rod Westerway's mount, passed in front of his own chest and smashed into Fred Onslow. Dan had actually seen none of those things yet he was aware that the nearest horse had shrieked with pain, reared, turned and stamped like a bucking bronco at a rodeo. Rod Westerway was trying to control it but it barged into Sim Taylor's horse before bounding across the yard, shaking its head fiercely to free itself of pain.

Dan couldn't remember casting any look in Fred Onslow's direction but he was aware that he was badly injured. Perhaps, he later surmised, out of the corner of his eye he'd seen him slump forward on to his horse's neck, but all he could remember was fixing his gaze on Carl Benton, whose yelled profanity made it clear that he, too, was reaching for a gun. It would have been logical for Dan to regard Sim Taylor as his first target: the cowboy already had his gun in his hand, but Dan chose the boss of the Flying B, whose gun was coming clear of leather.

He had no explanation for having been able, that day, to draw his gun so quickly: self-preservation, he supposed, because it was in his hand without any conscious thought of his drawing it. The two bullets that he put into Carl Benton's chest hurled him on to his back on the high veranda. Dan could hear the drumming of the dying man's feet as he turned his attention to Sim Taylor.

It was Rod Westerway's barging horse that had made it possible for Dan to tackle Carl Benton first. In its painful frenzy it had collided with Sim Taylor's mount, thereby making it impossible for that rider to fire another shot with any accuracy. By the time he had the chance of a clear shot at the deputy his boss was dead and the gun that had killed Benton was now pointing in his direction. His eyes widened: it was the last movement he made alive. Two slugs smashed into his chest and he was hurled from his horse on to the hard, dry ground.

Dan turned in the saddle and fired a shot at the fleeing Rod Westerway. He missed but didn't give chase. Westerway hadn't drawn his gun, hadn't become involved in the fight; it was more important to attend to Fred Onslow. It was a bad wound, one that needed Doc Pope's attention. With the aid of some of the Flying B crew he got the sheriff into a buggy and headed for Beecher Gulch.

# CHAPTER ELEVEN

In common with everyone else in the yard of the Flying B, Rod Westerway's attention had been fixed on the confrontation between Sheriff Onslow and his boss, so when the bullet from Sim Taylor's unexpected gunshot clipped off a portion of his horse's ear he was unprepared for its reaction. His first concerns were to stay aboard the animal and endeavour to control it, both of which he eventually achieved but not before the distressed animal had bolted to the far side of the compound.

From behind came the rattle of gunshots accompanied by the groans and cries of wounded and dying men. One look over his shoulder was sufficient to convince him that he should keep riding. Sim Taylor's horse was riderless, its owner lay in an untidy heap at its side. Carl Benton lay outstretched on the porch and the sheriff clung unsteadily to his horse. The deputy sat twisted in his saddle and it was only then that Rod realized that the lawman's gun was pointed in his direction.

The bullet, when it was fired, flew harmlessly wide and no more followed. Conscious that the deputy was more concerned about the wounded sheriff, Rod put spurs to his horse's flanks and rode away from the ranch house.

A few yards beyond the compound fence he pulled his horse to a halt. In his mind he debated his actions. He had no reason to flee from the ranch, he told himself; he was guilty of nothing more than being Carl Benton's foreman. Now that the initial outburst of violence was at an end it was probable that the lawmen would be prepared to listen to any evidence he had to impart about recent events.

Then he thought about the deputy and his gunman reputation, which could no longer be in doubt. He chose to let more time elapse before surrendering himself to the law.

Blood still escaped from the horse's ear and Rod Westerway knew that it needed to be treated quickly to avoid infection, but he had neither the means to attend to it out on the open range nor the desire to return to the ranch. He bathed the wound with water from his canteen, then considered his next move. He had decided to seek out a spot from which he could observe the ranch and await the departure of the lawmen when a troubling thought occurred to him. Jim Ford.

If the sheriff had already arrested one of the men brought from Cheyenne then a hunt would be on to find the others, and Rod's own part in the hiring of those men would be revealed. He couldn't claim that

146

they were brought in as extra hands on the ranch because they had camped several miles away. Even though he'd had no part in the attempt to lynch Carter and Potter he couldn't deny knowledge of the plot.

How the law would punish him if that became known was something he didn't wish to discover, but he knew the effect it would have on the other ranch hands. Such brutal disloyalty would not be tolerated and few would stay at the Flying B to work under a foreman who condoned that iniquitous behaviour. His only course of action was to warn Ford and his men that a posse was probably searching for them and that they needed to leave the territory immediately.

That, coupled with the news that Carl Benton was either dead or in the hands of the law proved to be sufficient inducement for Ford and his men to break camp and flee. Cut off from the source of income that had lured them to Wyoming, there was nothing to remain for. Seb Dutton had acted alone by remaining in Beecher Gulch when Ford and his men had returned to their camp so, if he had been captured, he had to face the consequences alone. Every man who rode wild faced the same risk.

Before Rod Westerway returned to the Flying B, Dan Freemont had reached Beecher Gulch and deposited the wounded sheriff into the doctor's care. From there, Dan hurried up the hillside to impart the news of her husband's injury to Annie Onslow. After driving her and Cora to the doctor's house Dan left the borrowed buggy at the livery stable and went along the street to the sheriff's office. His arrival in town had, of course, been witnessed by several people and news of the sheriff's injury had spread like wildfire. He was on the verge of relating the events at the Flying B to Zach Hartnell when they were joined by an anxious Theo Dawlish.

'What do we do now?' the store owner asked when Dan had told all.

'I understood you had plans to call in the army in such circumstances.' Dan replied.

Theo Dawlish waved aside that notion.

'That was at the prospect of civil unrest, a range war, but I suspect your action this morning has averted those. No, we're just a little town in need of someone to uphold the law until our sheriff is fit again.' The look he fixed on Dan made his meaning clear.

Dan shook his head but with less decisiveness than any previous rejections had held.

'I'm not sure how much longer I'll be staying here.'

As staunch in principles as he was strong in body, Zach Hartnell rarely compromised once his position on a topic had been determined. Since Dan's arrival in Beecher Gulch Zach had regarded him with suspicion, although he had no grounds for believing he was anything other than what he claimed: a wanderer hoping to make his fortune in Virginia City.

If Zach had examined his suspicions more closely he might have found that what troubled him most was the freedom with which Dan had attached himself to Sarah Riddle, and although he readily accepted that he was concerned for the widow he would have vehemently denied that his suspicions about Dan were caused by jealousy. He was a God-fearing citizen who acted strictly according to his creed of right and wrong and amorous thoughts for a recently bereaved woman could not be allowed to surface; they belonged to the devil's own. However, over the past few days his attitude towards Dan had shifted. The effort he'd put into fighting the fire had been the breakthrough, which was enhanced by the assistance he'd given Fred Onslow in the arrest of Carter and Potter and, later, the determination he'd shown against the lynch mob. Perhaps, he mused, he was the kind of man that was needed in Beecher Gulch.

'You can't go until the judge has tried those men in the cells,' he said. 'Your testimony will be essential if Fred isn't fit enough to attend the trial. Keep the badge until then and decide after that.'

Mention of the judge reminded Dan that he was due on the westbound train. His desire to be at the station when it arrived was, of course, not for that reason alone. Despite all that had happened in the few days he'd been in Beecher Gulch he hadn't forgotten the reason for his being there. Until the US marshal arrived his life was on hold and he remained a wanted man in danger of being exposed as a killer at any moment.

The office door opened. Linda Fellowes, trim and attractive in a yellow and black outfit entered. The troubled frown she wore disappeared when she saw Dan.

'I heard that there had been some trouble,' she said. 'I'm pleased you haven't been hurt.'

'The sheriff wasn't so lucky.' Dan gave her a summary of Fred Onslow's wound, then picked up his hat and headed for the door. 'I need to meet the judge from the train,' he explained.

Linda Fellowes offered to accompany him but the door opened again before they could leave the office. Cora Onslow regarded the people gathered there, her eyes lingering longest on Linda Fellowes. She brought the news that her father was in a lot of pain but it was a wound that would heal.

'My father wants to see you,' she told Dan.

The doctor had prepared a draught to combat the pain but once administered it would also put the patient to sleep. Dan's visit, therefore, had to be imme-diate, which meant delegating the task of meeting the judge to Theo Dawlish.

'You'll find the prisoners' confessions in the desk,' Dan told Theo. 'Give them to the judge and tell him I'll visit him at the hotel later.'

Barely a minute passed between the departure of Dan and Cora and the sounding of the train's whistle as it reached the outskirts of town. Theo Dawlish pulled open the top drawer of the desk in search of the required documents but stopped in amazement before sorting through the articles within. The top item was a newspaper and the face depicted on the front was that of the man who had walked out of the office only moments earlier. He put the newspaper on the desk and his muttered, 'A killer,' drew the attention of Zach Hartnell and Linda Fellowes.

'I haven't had the chance to thank you for sending your father to the jail last night,' Dan Freemont said to Cora as they walked towards the doctor's house. 'He arrived just in time.'

'I wasn't sure it was necessary,' she replied. 'I didn't know my father had appointed two deputies.'

'Two? Oh! you mean Linda Fellowes. Like me, she's a stranger in town, but she hasn't had the good fortune to be befriended by a good family. She needed company and a game of cards.'

'She obviously likes your company. She wouldn't give it up even with a lynch mob braying at the door.'

'It wasn't my idea, but I didn't have time to argue with her.'

'And today?'

'She'd heard about the shooting and was making enquiries about your father.'

Cora's glance registered her doubt about the accuracy of that answer, but none the less it served to soften her expression and her pursed lips eased into a smile.

'I have to thank you for bringing my father back to town. If you hadn't been with him the outcome could have been very different. Perhaps it wouldn't have been Carl Benton who was killed.'

'Are we friends then?' asked Dan. 'Can I look forward to another supper invitation?'

'Does it have to include your shadow?'

'It doesn't have to but it would be a neighbourly gesture.' That answer induced another sideways glance that marked her confusion about his relationship with the other woman. 'I don't know how long she's staying in Beecher Gulch,' he added, 'but I can assure you that her presence here has nothing to do with me.'

Cora's father was clearly in pain, his face grey and his eyes, watery and grey, were shrunk into narrow slits. They were alone in a small room that was almost filled by the single cot on which Fred Onslow lay.

'Try to delay the trial until I can attend,' he told Dan, 'or bring the judge here so that I can talk to him. Do what you can to plead for leniency for Carter and Potter. There's not much in their character to recommend them, but the information they gave us was vital to averting a range war. More innocent people would have died if we hadn't got Benton first.'

'I'll do what I can,' Dan promised

The sheriff grabbed his arm. 'I'd appreciate it if you stayed on as deputy until I'm back on my feet.'

'That might not be up to me. It will depend on what the US marshal tells me.'

'Is he here?'

'I don't know, but the train has arrived.'

Dan was conscious of the need to relieve Zach Hartnell, who had spent several hours that day keeping watch over the prisoners in the town jail. The blacksmith, he figured, would be eager to get back to his anvil. The Bright Star, however, was on his route from the doctor's house and a room had been reserved there for the judge. Making an early call on the judge provided him with the opportunity to discover if anyone else had registered there since the arrival of the train.

He looked up the street and could see that the jail-house door was closed and that there was little activity on the street. A group of men were gathered on the boardwalk opposite the jail but they were lounging against posts or sitting on rails like carefree cowherd-ers around a campfire. One of the men looked his way and another turned to study him, but in the shade of the building and with their hats low on their heads the distance was too great to identify them. He ignored them and went into the hotel.

Dan's disappointment on finding that the only new name penned into the register was that of Judge Arthur Barber was matched by his curiosity at the offhand manner in which Theo Dawlish addressed him as he descended the stairs across the short foyer.

'He's in number 8.' Without pausing the storekeeper left the hotel.

Dan had almost reached the top of the stairs when the street door burst open and a man stepped hur-riedly inside with a second man close on his heels. Dan paused to study them and figured they could have been two of the group who had been across the street from the jail.

The first was tall and dressed in dark range clothes. He was clearly confused by the absence of a clerk behind the desk. He stood in the centre of the foyer, turning left and right, looking for anyone or anything that might assist them in their purpose. The second man was shorter, stockier and the manner in which he moved his shoulders when he walked struck a familiar note. Like a good hunter, his senses were attuned to his surroundings. He raised his head to regard the figure at the top of the stairs and his twisted lip curled with satisfaction. His hand was grasping the butt of his pistol as he shouted his jubilation.

'There he is!'

Although he'd lived with the risk of discovery for several days, the sight of Jason Whalley's men took Dan Freemont completely by surprise. He thought he had lost them, bamboozled them, tricked them into believing he was east or south of Scottsbluff. Recognition, he'd imagined, would have been the result of Wanted posters or newspaper articles. Yet here they were and he was looking directly into the eyes of the man he'd fought in the Scottsbluff stable.

Even though those thoughts had come and gone in a split second they hampered his response, and by the time he moved it was too late to go for his gun. Seb Dutton's weapon was almost clear of his holster and Dan's only course of action was to throw himself full length into the corridor to his left. Below, a gun barked and a jagged lump of plaster was blasted from the wall at the top of the stairs.

Scrabbling, using hands and knees to propel himself forward, Dan aimed for the turning at the far end of the corridor, which led to his own room. He could hear footsteps on the stairs and from below the irate shouting of the hotel manager. In the confines of the corridor the next shot fired seemed to be directly behind Dan's head. The bullet tugged his shirt as he made the safety of the corner.

By now Dan had drawn his Colt and sent an answering shot back along the corridor he'd vacated. Someone cursed but nothing in the voice conveyed pain, so Dan assumed his bullet had not found a target.

A door opened and an austere voice demanded to know what was happening. When the speaker was told to get back in his room he announced he was Judge Arthur Barber and he demanded that the shooting stop immediately. The sounds that followed left Dan in no doubt that the judge had been gun-whipped and now lay unconscious on the floor.

At the far end of the corridor that Dan now occupied was a door which led down to a rear alley. In his mind he was debating whether to use that as an escape route or to seek sanctuary in his own room. There was no certainty of reaching either and although his own room was closer he knew that the door was locked.

An arm appeared around the corner and the gun in its hand spat flame and lead which flew high over Dan's head. He replied with two well-aimed shots that saw the hasty withdrawal of the arm as the gun clattered to the floor. No effort was made to collect the dropped weapon and the agony in the wounded man's groans indicated the pain he was suffering. With one assailant out of the fray, Dan squatted behind a low table and awaited the second man.

Seb Dutton, the man with the twisted lip, peered cautiously around the corner. Unable to see Dan, suspecting he'd gone into one of the rooms, he stepped fully into the corridor. Reluctant to shoot him without warning, Dan called for him to throw away the gun. He didn't. He reacted with the speed of a rattlesnake, twisting towards the direction of the voice and firing as he did so. His bullet removed a chunk of wood from the table but missed Dan. Dan didn't miss. The first shot hit Dutton in the chest, spun him round as his hands clutched at the hole that had been made there. The second shot lifted him off his feet and he crashed to the floor, dead.

Dan hurried to where the body lay and caught a glimpse of the wounded man who was making his escape via the stairs. Dan's mind was full of thoughts of pursuit but behind him a door opened and, casting a backward glance, he realized that the fight wasn't over. Following the sound of gunfire, another two men had used the stairs at the back of the hotel and were closing on him.

Pressing himself against the wall, using the corner for immediate protection, Dan fired a shot towards his new assailants, but when he squeezed the trigger again it fell on an empty cylinder. He was out of bullets and without any hope of refilling the Colt. He could hear the footfalls as the men approached the corner. Then, unexpectedly, a voice shouted a command.

'Put down those weapons.' The authority to issue

that demand was confirmed in the shouted identification: 'US marshal.'

A moment of silence followed, then a gun roared twice to advertise the fact that the gunmen had chosen to disobey the order. Gatt Harding staggered backwards, his knees, sagged and he folded on to the corridor's floor to die beside Seb Dutton. The second man was alive but moaning in agony as he lay curled on the floor, his knees drawn up as though trying to stop his innards from spilling out of his body. Blood saturated his shirt and hands. Over him, smoking revolver in hand, stood Linda Fellowes.

'US marshal?' queried Dan.

'I've been looking for you,' she said.

'Why are you posing as a gambler?' Dan asked.

'Why are you posing as a deputy?'

Despite her shotgun support at the jail when the mob had been determined to lynch Potter and Carter, and poker skills that were little above basic, the thought that Linda Fellowes was the US marshal for whom Dan been waiting had never occurred to him. He was, of course, aware that the government had used female agents during and after the war, but that, he had supposed, was in the East where the mores of civilization were different. So, when the bodies had been removed from the hotel, the judge and the wounded man had been attended to by Doctor Pope, and they were alone, his gratitude for her latest intervention was forced to take second place. Her masquerade, he complained, had led him to doubt that a marshal would ever arrive in Beecher Gulch and that he would forever be a wanted man.

It was Linda's argument that adopting the guise of a gambler gave her the freedom to talk with Dan Freemont without arousing the interest of anyone else in town. What could be more natural than fellow gamblers facing each other across a card table? But his use of a different name and acting like a well-established town deputy had deceived her; she'd only learned his true identity when her attention was drawn to the newspaper in the sheriff's office.

Eventually they acknowledged the humour of the situation and Dan told his story about the Scottsbluff killing.

'And that's the truth,' he ended.

Linda's first words surprised Dan. 'We always knew that you didn't kill Henry Garland,' she told him. 'Your friend, Robert Halliday, waited at the foot of the stairs for you. He testified that you were in the corridor when the shot was fired. Perhaps we shouldn't have allowed the press to print Jason Whalley's version of events, but I don't think it would have altered anything. His men would still have been under orders to find you.'

'So you don't want me back in Nebraska?'

'Not until a trial date is set. We'll need your testimony.' She paused, picked up the old Wanted poster that he'd carried with him since that night.

'Archie Baker! Are you sure he's the same man?'

With his affirmation, Linda announced that she

would send a telegram to her superiors that would see Jason Whalley arrested before nightfall.

Two days later Dan escorted Linda Fellowes to the station to catch the eastbound train. The previous night they'd been invited to supper at the sheriff's home, where Fred Onslow had been almost as pleased as Cora to see Dan. Although still weak, the news that Dan wasn't leaving Beecher Gulch any time soon was a boost to the sheriff's recovery, especially when he agreed to stay on as deputy.

'What about Mrs Riddle's place?' Fred asked. 'I thought you intended helping out there.'

'Zack Hartnell offered to stand in for me. I think that sort of work suits him better than sitting guard in the jail house.'

'Well,' said Annie Onslow, who had offered little to the conversation but interjected with an insight that had escaped the men in the room, 'if any man deserves a good wife it's Zach.'

But it was a phrase that Linda Fellowes had kept tucked in her mind until she stepped on to the boarding plate at the back of the carriage. Dan had been asking her about her arrival in Beecher Gulch, if the incident that had played out when she left the train had been staged to establish her cover as a gambler. Her answer was vague, tantalizing, which left Dan no wiser for asking.

'I'm just pleased you're not a professional gambler,' he told her. 'If we'd played for real money the night we were interrupted you'd be going home with an empty purse.'

She laughed, revealing a strong jawline which he admired. He gave her his hand to help her on to the train.

'I hope we meet again,' he said.

'Perhaps we will,' she answered, 'but now that you're a genuine lawman, perhaps there's a good wife for you, too.'